The Heirs of the
MEDALLION
BOOK FIVE

RICARDO

David Sage

The Heirs of the Medallion: RICARDO
Copyright © 2018 by Mr. Sage's Stories

For information about this title or to order other books and/or electronic media, contact the publisher:
Mr. Sage's Stories
www.mrsagesstories.com

ISBN: 978-0-9894210-8-9

Printed in the United States of America

Cover and Interior design by: 1106 Design

With Thanks

To our friends of more than 40 years in Mexico, whose names I've used in this book, I cherish the memories of our times together!

To Robbie for faithfully supporting the Medallion series in your bookstore, someday I might make it to the top shelf!

To readers from 8 to 80 who have followed the medallion's history, I hope the final book meets your expectations!

Finally, to my family: Marcia, Dave, Tierney, and Ty, for your incalculable contributions and support throughout this process. I love you all.

David Sage
Story, Wyoming

Table of Contents

Foreword

IN MID-JUNE OF 1997, Juan and Sophia Valdez, 12 year-old twins from Center, Colorado, were given three unusual items by their great-grandfather. The first was a five-foot long Incan sling. The second was a cloth shirt of almost impenetrable Incan armor. The third was an ancient silver medallion from the Inca Empire.

The use of the sling and armor has been a family tradition for 500 years. The medallion, passed down from generation to generation, holds a great secret, which the family will one day discover. Great Grandfather instructs them to look through the square hole in the medallion at the rising sun on the Summer Solstice. When they do, the twins view a skirmish between Incan warriors and conquistadors. Great Grandfather then begins the epic tale of the family's history with the medallion, which began with that battle.

The first book in the series, **Adzul,** recounts the story of a young warrior's flight through the Andes to save the medallion. Pursued by conquistadors, he is nearly killed several times before making his way through Central America months later. Just when he thinks he's safe, he encounters other conquistadors bent on pillaging the Aztec Empire.

The second book, **Cuto,** chronicles the story of Adzul's grandson, who leaves his village to seek adventure in new town of Santa Fe far to the north. Befriended by Pueblo Indians, Cuto and his companions are forced into hiding when a sadistic soldier determines to slay him.

Lita picks up the narrative more than 60 years later. She and her brother Rutu set out to find the Great Water in the northwest, talked about by traders bringing ivory carvings to trade with the Pueblo Indians. Brutal winter conditions stop them in the far north. To avoid starvation, they join Crow Indian friends in a desperate hunt for The Beast.

Book four, **Tukor,** is the story of Lita's great, great grandson. More than a century after her journey, he rescues an Inuit man enslaved by the Comanche and together they travel to the Pacific Northwest. Fascinated by the sea, Tukor takes part a whale hunt that ends in disaster.

The conclusion to the series is **Ricardo,** in which Great Grandfather reveals his astonishing past to Juan and Sophia and joins them in the discovery of the medallion's ancient secret.

Family Wearers of the Medallion	Friends of the Family
Qist Incan warrior (Circa 1540) |	
Adzul Son of Qist, married Itta (Aztec) (Circa 1540–1612) |	**Quauhtli,** Itta's brother **Yaoti,** warrior
Cuto Grandson of Adzul, married Ria (Circa 1590–1680) |	**Feather,** Pueblo chief **Swallow,** Feather's daughter **Walks in the Grass,** warrior **Backward Looking,** warrior
Lita Granddaughter of Cuto, sister of Rutu (Circa 1650–1740) |	**Badger Snarling,** Ute warrior **Knows No Fear,** Crow chief **Chattering Squirrel,** Crow boy – renamed **Beast Blinder**
Ria II Granddaughter of Lita, married Sand, the great, great grandson of Swallow (Circa 1710–1805) |	
Tukor Grandson of Ria II (Circa 1785–1895) |	**Tikaani,** Inuit ex-slave **Qimmiq,** Tikaani's father **Hatch,** Makah chief **Talon,** harpooner
Ricardo Great grandson of Tukor, married Martha (Circa 1895–2003) |	**Rodriguez** family: Jorge, Anna, Christa, Bruno, Gissy **Rock Dog,** Ute Indian, and **Gabby,** his wife.
Juan and Sophia Great grandchildren of Ricardo (Circa 1982–)	

CHAPTER 1
Solstice

IT WAS STILL DARK IN Center, Colorado, as Juan padded down the hall to his sister's room unconsciously touching the medallion hanging from his neck. It was circular, four inches in diameter, and had strange markings inscribed on front and back. In the middle was a square hole, one inch to a side. Made from solid silver, it should have been heavy enough to cause strain on the back of his neck, but it was strangely light, so much so he usually forgot he was wearing it. Furthermore, despite having been worn continuously by members of his family for more than 500 years, its surface wasn't tarnished and the markings were as sharply etched in the metal as the day they were made. As far as he knew, its leather strap had never been replaced.

As he reached the door to his twin's room, Juan was thinking that it was only the peculiarities of birth that rendered him Wearer of the medallion: he had emerged into the world a scant 30 seconds after his sister and the silver was always passed to the youngest member of the family. After the fashion of identical twins who are extremely close, he often wished she had arrived second so she could experience the honor of bearing the wonderful piece of silver.

It had been created in the Inca Empire sometime after Pizarro led the Spanish conquistadors into the country. When the invaders executed Emperor Atahualpa, despite his having a room filled with gold for them to pay his own ransom, his most trusted advisor Qist had escaped with his son to a secret city high in the Andes Mountains. Years passed before the Spanish accidentally stumbled on the city and attacked. In the ensuing battle, Qist was mortally wounded. As he lay dying, he handed the medallion to his now 20-year-old son Adzul with instructions to keep it out of the hands of the conquistadors and flee the Empire. He said the piece of silver possessed a great secret that someday would be revealed to the family.

Pursued by five soldiers with murderous intent, Adzul barely escaped into the Amazon Basin. Months later, after many harrowing brushes with death, he reached the Aztec Empire in Mexico, only to encounter new conquistadors savagely bent on destroying that nation. With the help of his new wife and their warrior friends, a trap was set and the danger eradicated, but the village was forced to relocate to the northern wilderness of the Empire. At last he could settle down, secure in the knowledge the medallion was safe.

Decades later, Adzul's grandson took the medallion north to Santa Fe where he and his wife became horse trainers in a remote desert canyon. During the ensuing centuries, the medallion traveled with Adzul's descendants to many locations, from the remote Comanche Empire in eastern Texas to vast reaches north of the Arctic Circle. It always alerted its Wearer to danger and manifested mysterious powers that protected and saved each of them from deadly peril. But it wasn't until Great Grandfather gave the medallion to Juan and Sophia, two years earlier, that its greatest magic was revealed. Following Qist's ancient instructions, the twins had dutifully looked through the square hole at the rising sun on the morning of the Summer Solstice. For more than five centuries family members had done the same thing, to no avail. On that June 21st morning, however, everything changed: a scene from the past materialized before the twins' astonished eyes. On each succeeding Solstice, winter and summer, the medallion revealed something from its history. Using the scenes as a starting point, Great Grandfather had traced the family's history with the medallion in a series of stories, usually told to the twins over Saturday breakfasts at his house.

Now it was June 21st again. Dawn was less than an hour away and sunrise not long after that. Juan had woken long before his alarm went off, filled with excitement. He was now a slender, but powerfully built, 14-year-old and, like his sister, a superb student/athlete/outdoorsman. He reached for the doorknob, only to see the door swing open.

"Couldn't sleep either?" whispered Sophia through the dark.

"No, I thought we could have coffee and one of those apple cinnamon muffins Mom made while we wait," he replied softly.

"Great idea," she breathed, stepping past him into the hall.

CHAPTER 2

Stonemason

TWO HOURS LATER THEY WERE standing on the lawn in front of the house staring at the Sangre de Cristo Mountains to the east. The familiar jagged peaks still had snow filling the deep canyons and ravines along their steep sides, creating a stunning perspective against the backdrop of blue sky...even though the mountains were nearly 30 miles away. The brilliant orb of the sun was making its way slowly into the sky from behind the peaks; as it cleared the last summit the twins, heads together, stared at it through the medallion. For an instant nothing happened, then the familiar black smoke blew across the hole.

When it cleared, they saw a man bent low over the corner of a rectangular slab of rock elevated waist-high by stacks of stone blocks under each corner. In one hand, the man held a wooden mallet and in the other a shaft of black rock eight inches long and tapered to a point. He angled the pointed rock carefully to a spot on the slab and gave it a series of three quick blows with the mallet, then leaned close to examine the result. Apparently satisfied, he repositioned the stone tool and struck it three times again. The twins could clearly hear a "clink" each time he hit the shaft and see tiny chips fly from the slab.

"That's a chisel," muttered Juan. "He's carving something into that slab."

"It's a pattern," said Sophia. "He's cutting away the rock to leave a raised pattern on the surface at the corner of the block. Can you see it? …Oh my gosh, look at that!" Suddenly, black smoke rolled across the scene and the familiar houses of Center came back into focus through the medallion's hole.

"I'm telling you, Great Grandfather, it was a circular pattern with a raised square section sticking up in the middle. The little square post looked to be just the size of the hole in the medallion!" Sophia could hardly get the words out fast enough.

It was 8:00 AM and the twins were on Great Grandfather's front porch, surrounded by flower pots, coffee and fresh blueberry scones on the table before them. Their relative was sitting in a beautiful handmade rocking chair, mug of coffee in hand. Dressed in jeans, light wool shirt, and soft work boots, his brown face and lively eyes gave no indication that he was nearly 102 years old.

"Slow down, slow down," he grinned. "What was the setting?" The twins looked at each other in confusion.

"Well," said Juan slowly, "it was outdoors, but the scene was so focused on the man that I didn't notice much else. Except," he suddenly brightened, "I did notice tools scattered about on the ground, several large chisels and mallets; a couple of the chisels had flat blades, not points. It was sunny and there might have been a hill in the background."

"It was over so fast," added Sophia. "Faster than any scene we've observed before. But it was clear that the man was being very careful, studying the pattern before he placed the chisel point down."

"The design was circular?" asked the old man.

"Definitely," replied Sophia.

"What was the man wearing?" Again, the twins stared at each other.

"A woolen cap," Sophia began.

"Sleeveless belted tunic reaching his knees," added Juan.

"Uncu," murmured Great Grandfather.

"Sandals," said Juan. "There might have been a long cloak thrown over a nearby pile of stone blocks."

"Yacolla," muttered the old man.

"Oh, he had big yellow plugs in his earlobes," stated Sophia with conviction.

"That's my sister," grinned Juan. "She'll pick up on the jewelry!" There was silence for a moment as the twins searched their memories. They looked at Great Grandfather apologetically.

"Sorry," sighed Sophia. "There wasn't time to take in much more."

"The two of you have amazing powers of observation," stated Great Grandfather to their astonishment. "How long did the scene last?"

"Less than a minute," said Juan as Sophia nodded in agreement. "What was it about?" he asked. The old man's answer shocked them.

"I have absolutely no idea," he replied, taking a sip of coffee.

"But, surely…?" Juan's voice trailed off. Great Grandfather smiled.

"What you saw was not about one of our family members and the medallion, as far as I know. The man was clearly Inca, due to the clothes and earplugs, but perhaps the vision predates Adzul's escape, since we know everything that happened to him after Qist died. From your description, it seems the man was creating an image on the stone block that bears resemblance to the medallion, but nothing in the family history addresses such a scene."

"But, do you think it relates to the medallion?" pressed Juan.

"Perhaps," replied Great Grandfather. "The square feature in the center of the pattern is certainly intriguing."

"For two years, every scene we looked at through the medallion has progressed forward through time," noted Sophia. "If this one took place before Adzul, what do you think it means?"

"I wish I knew," said the old man.

CHAPTER 3

Birth and Death

THE MORNING SUN highlighted the dark, polished wood of the deck and the air was pleasantly cool. A bee buzzed among the colorful riot of reds, purples, and yellows overflowing the hanging plants, stopping from time to time to make its way down into a blossom. It was a week later and Great Grandfather was settled comfortably in his rocking chair, staring fondly at the twins sitting in folding canvas chairs before him. Breakfast had been a grand affair of fried eggs, blueberry pancakes, and sausage, during which the twins lamented the fact that last week's strange view into the past offered no opportunity for Great Grandfather to continue the story about their ancestors.

"We thought there might be a scene from Tukor's trip to the Arctic," Juan had said. "We've no idea about what happened to him."

"I will get to that in time, but first I thought I might describe how I came to the Valley," replied the old man. "After all, I'm not going to live forever and the two of you are now custodians of the family history. You should know what happened to the previous Wearer." The twins settled back, eyes sparkling. This promised to be interesting because, apart from the few details he'd shared about his involvement with Mrs. Martinez, they really had no knowledge of his life other than some vague references by their father that the old man had a colorful past.

"I was born in one of the three original little houses Cuto built when he settled in the hidden canyon. My mother died in the delivery..." he began.

The baby's squalling was accompanied by an anguished cry in the dark outside, as one of the midwives delivered the tragic news to the young father that his wife had died giving birth to their first child. The devastated husband rushed in and knelt to clasp his wife's body to his chest, tears running down his cheeks. Moments went by as he rocked back and forth whispering her name. At last he gently laid her down and turned toward the woman holding the baby. A tender smile emerged as he bent to stare at the tiny red face.

"You arrived at such a price, little one," he murmured. "But what are we to do with you?" He raised his eyes questioningly to the midwife.

"We'll find a woman in the village to come and take care of him," the older woman said reassuringly.

"Him? Ahh, it's a boy! I didn't think to ask."

"In this moment your thoughts are with your wife," she said. "But, yes, you have a fine young son. There will be many women eager to help raise him."

As dawn flooded the sky with orange, Carlos carried the blanket-wrapped body of his beloved wife to the far end of the valley. Along the bottom of the towering cliffs was a neat line of stone covered mounds: the final resting place for Cuto, Ria, Tepin, Necalli, Lita, Rutu, and other family members who had lived their lives in these remote canyons. Nearby, hidden by a thick growth of bushes, was the low entrance to a cave. Inside, the Ancient Ones had painted many scenes on the walls and a hidden shaft gave access to the desert above.

The man worked slowly and deliberately, letting memories wash over him. When he finished several hours later, a matching grave had been added to the others. He lingered for long minutes, talking aloud to his wife as though she was standing beside him, before starting back along the beautiful stream emerging from the base of the cliffs. Every so often he would whistle sharply, veer from the shade of the cottonwoods flanking the creek, and approach a group of horses grazing nearby. Singling out one of Isabella's favorites, he would spend time rubbing its neck and murmuring in a soft voice before resuming his walk down valley. It was midday when he finally reached the houses.

The next morning a young woman named Rose arrived with her family to take care of the baby. She had an infant herself, and two young children who filled the cluster of gardens and little houses with laughter and shouts. Her husband, an excellent gardener and horse trainer, worked side-by-side with Carlos and sought unsuccessfully to take his mind off the tragedy. Carlos and Isabella had planned together to adjust the specialties of their horse herd to the growing demand for accomplished animals to work with cattle. Buffalo were long gone and the days of the Indian wars over, but the same agility and speed Ria had taught buffalo runners and war horses was as much in demand as ever, just for different applications. Isabella's death, however, sapped Carlos' enthusiasm and for a while he left much of the horse training to others.

Only his baby Ricardo, growing chubby under Rose's excellent care, could take his mind off the loss of his wife. At the end of two months, he had Rose fashion a small blanket fitted with a cloth strap so that he could carry his son across his chest. Despite her protests, he smoothly vaulted aboard one of his most gentle horses and headed up the canyon at a slow walk. The unexpected and abrupt motion of mounting prompted loud wailing, but before long the easy movement of the horse's gait soothed the child. When they returned, 30 minutes later, the baby was waving fat arms and cooing at the sky while Carlos was wrinkling his nose at a rather strong smell from his little bundle. He hastily handed the child to Rose before dismounting!

From that time forward Carlos rode twice a day with little Ricardo, returning him to Rose for food and naps. In later years she said the boy learned to ride before he learned to crawl and, in large measure, she was correct. At one he was sitting in front of Carlos on the horse and at two he was astride his own horse, being led by his father. Before he was three, Carlos fashioned a miniature sling for him and by the time he was four he was able to throw a rock accurately from horseback.

Teaching riding skills to his son reawakened Carlos' interest in training horses and he began to involve himself more fully with the management of the herds. When Ricardo was five, an older man from the village in the main canyon approached Carlos one day.

"A Mexican named Rodriguez has built a hacienda in the desert many miles beyond the entrance to our canyon," he said. "He's diverted water from a small river to make grassland for cattle. When I was in Santa Fe for supplies last week, he approached and asked about the alertness and powerful build of my horse. When I explained, he said he'd heard about horses trained in a remote canyon but thought it was a legend. He needs skilled animals and wondered whether we could come and give a demonstration at his hacienda."

CHAPTER 4
Hacienda

THREE WEEKS LATER Carlos and four riders topped a low rise and paused in astonishment, letting the herd of 25 horses meander on before them. Several miles ahead a large patch of green shown like a vast emerald in the middle of the parched desert.

"What is that?" asked the five-year-old boy astride a pinto next to his father.

"It must be the hacienda Armando told me about," answered Carlos without taking his eyes from the sight. The man we're going to see has redirected water from a river to grow grass in the desert, just like we do at home to water the gardens," he added. The boy nodded, sitting his horse as naturally as though he were part of the animal. He rode bareback, except for a colorful blanket pad under his hips.

"That must be the place," said Armando, easing his horse alongside father and son. "I had no idea he'd created so much grassland."

"Let's go meet this man," replied Carlos, nudging his horse forward. "He must have big ideas to change the desert like that."

They had been leisurely trailing the little herd for three days, following the creek for miles down the main canyon until it entered the desert and turned north. From that point, their direction was east and each night they sought out springs and grass for the animals among the rocky hills. They moved slowly during daytime because of the desert heat, but now with their destination in sight the herd seemed to sense the men's curiosity and picked up the pace on its own. It was well past midday when they crossed a small ditch burbling with water and entered a great, open pasture with grass growing well above their horses' knees. Scattered across the landscape were brown cattle with white faces.

"These are not like the wild cattle we sometimes see in the desert," said Carlos. "Have you seen animals like these before?" he called to Armando.

"No, but the people in Santa Fe said Rodriguez was experimenting with different breeds of cattle," replied the older man.

When they came in sight of a cluster of buildings, Carlos nodded his head in approval. Before them was a collection of barns, sheds, bunkhouses, and corrals, bordered by a sizeable stream. On the other side of the creek was a grand two-story adobe home surrounded by flower beds and a wide grass border. What impressed him was the immaculate condition of the property; on a much larger scale, it reminded him of home. Men in wide-brimmed hats were working near the corrals and one waved his hand in greeting, then hurried to open the gate of a large pen. When the horses were safely inside he closed the gate and approached Carlos.

"The Patrón has been anxious to see your horses," he said. "I'm sure he has seen you coming and will be here shortly. Please let us take your mounts and care for them. They will be rubbed down and fed before we turn them loose with the others.

"Thank you," said Carlos as they all dismounted. "Is there water in the pen?"

"Yes, a ditch from the stream flows through it and we will fork hay in as well."

A shouted greeting caught the attention of the visitors. Striding across a bridge toward them was a man not much older than Carlos. He wore one of the wide hats they had become accustomed to seeing in Santa Fe, a colorful shirt, and belted pants covering cowboy boots. A wide smile split his face as he clasped Carlos' hand in greeting.

"I am Jorge Rodriguez. I've been looking forward to your visit!" he exclaimed. "Since I met Armando," he nodded toward the older man, "I've learned much about your family. Everyone knows the high caliber and training of your horses, but there's a strange reluctance to discuss your exact whereabouts. People say mysterious beings protect you and threaten anyone who comes near. That's why I told Armando I thought your family was just a legend." Now it was Carlos' turn to smile.

"There was a time when people wanted to steal our horses, but unusual circumstances put a stop to it," he answered enigmatically. Rodriguez raised his eyebrows in surprise and seemed about to say something, but thought the better of it and turned toward Ricardo.

"Is this your son?" He observed the headband, cotton blouse and pants, and knee-high moccasins. The lad, after the fashion of the men, was dressed like a Pueblo Indian but was clearly of a different race. "He rode all this way with you?"

"Yes, this is Ricardo. He was on a horse with me at two months old, and aboard a horse by himself since he was two years old."

"Your wife approves?"

"She died giving birth to him," said Carlos quietly.

"I'm so sorry," said their host, pausing respectfully before going on. "But I have a surprise for you, Ricardo. I have a son, Bruno, who's just five years old."

"I'm five too!" said the youngster.

"I wondered," replied the man. He turned to Carlos. "Will you and your son be our guests at the house? Your men will find comfortable accommodations in the bunkhouse," he gestured at a long building nearby, "and we all eat together in the dining hall."

"We gladly accept," replied Carlos, eying the large home. "We have clean clothes in our packs, but I'm afraid we're travel worn."

"I understand," said Rodriguez as they walked across the bridge. "We're often in the saddle for days at a time. We are lucky that three of the men's wives take care of all our clothes. After supper you can have a bath in the tub." Father and son exchanged a curious look.

"What's a tub?" piped up the boy.

"Oh, it's the most wonderful invention!" exclaimed their host. "It's like a big barrel cut sideways that you can fill with hot water and lots of soap. You can even stretch out full length," he laughed.

"We wash in the stream," announced Ricardo matter-of-factly.

"You're going to love a tub-bath," said the man as they approached the arched entry leading to an inner courtyard. A beautiful young woman in a long blue dress stepped forward to greet them. She had brown eyes and black hair. Beside her stood a tall older woman with gray hair and a wrinkled face. Both were smiling broadly; between them stood a boy the same size as Ricardo. He was dressed exactly like his father, minus the hat. Peeping out from behind him was a little girl no more than two years old, dressed in blue just like her mother.

"This is my wife Anna," explained Rodriguez, "my mother Christa, Bruno and Gissy."

"Welcome to our home," said the younger woman enthusiastically, going to one knee to address Ricardo. "Look at you! You came all this way with your father to visit us?"

"It was easy," he said seriously. "Our horses are strong and well trained."

"Want to see my model railroad?" interrupted Bruno. At Ricardo's nod, the two of them took off down a long hall, trailed by little Gissy.

CHAPTER 5
Bathtub

ONCE INSIDE, CARLOS realized the house was
built around a large interior courtyard. In the center
of the courtyard was an eight-foot statue of a girl on
tiptoes holding a large shell over her head. From the
shell water poured into a large basin at the statue's feet.
Around the fountain were scattered clusters of wooden
chairs and tables under large umbrellas. Stone plant-
ers filled with flowers were artfully placed among the
furniture and doors on all sides gave access from the
interior of the house.

"It's beautiful," he said to the three adults as they
looked out on the courtyard from a room furnished
with comfortable sofas and chairs. "Inside our canyons

we have many flower beds, but no fountains; only ditches which carry water to the gardens, but the sound is similar."

"We came from Mexico City a few years ago and the desert seemed so harsh we wanted to hear the sound of water," explained Anna.

"Mexico City...in Santa Fe they say it is very large," said Carlos. "Bigger than we can imagine."

"Yes, and very crowded," replied Jorge. "It began to encroach on the ranch my grandfather started 50 years ago, and the people didn't respect our livestock, so we sold it and moved to the open spaces of New Mexico."

"My family also moved from Mexico," said Carlos. "But in those days it was known as the Aztec Empire." The three stared at him in disbelief.

"You've been here that long?" asked the stunned rancher. "The Empire existed more than 300 years ago!"

"Yes. Perhaps someday I'll tell you the story, but it's a long one," answered Carlos. "My ancestors had some interesting experiences with the conquistadors."

"From the stories I've heard about your family, I'll bet they did!" exclaimed Rodriguez.

"I hate to interrupt," said Anna, "but the bell is ringing for supper. I'll go and collect the children."

The meal, conducted in the dining hall across the creek, was a loud and friendly affair. In addition to the Patrón and his family, there were 15 other families living and working at the hacienda, complete with kids of all ages. Three long rows of tables, with benches on both sides, barely accommodated the group. Unaccustomed to such a crowd in a confined space, Carlos observed that all the children were well-mannered and polite, despite the hubbub of voices. Bruno and Ricardo, already friends, sat together between Bruno's parents, Gissy close behind them in a high chair. Great platters of steaks, vegetables, tortillas, and refried beans were passed around and by the end of the meal hardly a scrap remained.

"Tomorrow we'd like to see you demonstrate the abilities of your horses," said Jorge as everyone moved outside to enjoy the cool of the evening.

"Of course," replied Carlos, "but may I ask why you need animals such as ours? Your white-faced cattle seem calm and placid."

"And they are," laughed his companion. "It's the range cattle we need good horses for. They're fast and wild as badgers, with extremely long horns they readily use against our mounts when chased. We've lost several horses to them'" he added somberly, "and nearly one rider."

"In the past our animals were used as buffalo runners," explained Carlos. "We still train them the same way even though the buffalo are gone. I think our horses could be useful to you in dealing with such cattle."

That night the visitors were treated to the wonderful experience of a warm bath. Three gleaming white bathtubs had been carefully brought from Mexico City. Each stood on four short, clawed legs. Drain pipes had been cleverly fashioned in the floor so water could be emptied after the bath. Bruno led the way confidently into the room containing one of the tubs, Ricardo trailing a bit behind. Quickly shedding his clothes, the young host trotted to the tub and climbed in. Anna grabbed the visitor's hand.

"Don't worry," she said softly. "It's really a lot of fun." When he was ready, she let him peer over the edge at the water. "Put your finger in it and see how good it feels," she encouraged. He did and glanced at her with a little smile.

"Get in!" encouraged Bruno, sitting chest deep and waving his arms back and forth under the surface.

"Ready?" asked Anna. At his hesitant nod, she lifted the boy carefully over the edge. "Sit down and get the feel of it." She placed two small wooden boats on the water, each with a little white sail. "Blow on the sails and watch what happens." The young guest just stared. The warm water was strange and wonderful and he'd never seen a sailboat.

"Watch!" exclaimed Bruno, bending forward and blowing gently on one of the boats. As it skittered away across the tub, Ricardo's eyes widened in amazement. Minutes later he puffed on the other boat and before long the two boys were laughing and playing with the boats like two otters. Anna knelt by the edge cautioning them about too much splashing, a wide smile on her face.

Later, when Ricardo was fast asleep in their big bed, Carlos quietly left their room and experienced the luxury of indoor bathing for himself.

CHAPTER 6

Horsemanship

Breakfast was a bit more subdued than dinner as the children were still sleepy, but piles of eggs, sausage, and flapjacks disappeared nonetheless. Afterward, the men headed for the pen containing the visiting horses. One by one, Carlos and his trainers walked slowly through the herd, selected a horse, slipped a hackamore over its head, and led it out. Finally, Ricardo entered the pen. He uttered a strange chirp and a pinto separated from the herd and walked to the boy. After being rewarded with a carrot, the horse bowed its head low enough for Ricardo to slip on its hackamore. The astonished ranch hands exchanged looks.

"We have to rope the horses we want to ride," explained Rodriguez to Carlos. "They're usually extremely skittish in the corral. Why do your horses remain so calm?"

"We work constantly with them. From the time they're foals they see us walking or riding quietly among them, talking and giving attention to the older horses. All the animals we brought love to run. But they also love to perform, and without a rider they can't, so they are eager for us to come and choose them." The rancher just shook his head. Never had he heard of such a thing; so far, it seemed that Carlos' family deserved its reputation.

"What was that noise you made?" Bruno asked Ricardo. The two boys were standing beside the pinto as Armando placed a small pad on its back.

"It was my call for this horse," explained Ricardo. "I'm too small to go into the herd and put on a bridal, so I call the horse to me. I have a different call for each of the four animals I ride. It helps to have a carrot though," he added with a grin.

"Don't you use a saddle?" asked Bruno. "We all ride in a saddle."

"No, we use these pads. But they're thick and comfortable," he hastened to explain, staring at the saddled horses being led from one of the barns. "Saddles look pretty hard for sitting on." He put a foot into Armando's cupped hands and vaulted aboard the pinto." Are you going to watch us ride?"

"Yes," cried the other boy, running toward a small gray horse being led from the barn. The ranch hand boosted him into the saddle and he trotted his horse over to Ricardo. "What are you going to do?"

"You'll see," replied Ricardo as they joined the group heading toward a nearby field.

For the next three hours Carlos and his men put each of the horses they'd brought through a series of exercises, ranging from weaving through complex patterns of rock they'd laid out, to figure-eights, to abrupt stops and reversals in direction, to backing the animals in a straight line for many yards. All demonstrations were conducted at full speed, with little or no apparent guidance from the rider. Well versed with ropes, the visitors even played a game where one rider did his best to race through a spacious course pursued by another horseman with a long braided lasso. Despite superb maneuvering to avoid capture, the speed and agility of the horses was such that the pursued rarely reached the finish line without feeling the long loop settle gently over his shoulders.

Ricardo participated in most of the exercises, clinging like a burr to three of the horses as they went through the demonstrations.

"That boy looks like he's a part of the horse," exclaimed Jorge, sitting on his mount beside Carlos.

"The animals are like family to us: for generations each child has been involved with them from an early age."

"Bruno's a good rider, but he couldn't do *that* bareback," the rancher shook his head.

"That's only because he was raised with a saddle," smiled his guest. "If all he knew was the pad, we would have two little boys glued to their horses."

"You may be right," chuckled the Patrón. "But I'd have a hard time trying to convince my son to switch now."

After lunch Rodriguez and 10 of his men were given canyon horses and set out with the four visitors to find some range cattle; Ricardo stayed behind to play with Bruno. Although Carlos and his men used only riding pads, they were well aware of market demands and all the horses had been schooled with saddles. The only difference they strictly adhered to was that all were ridden with hackamores; no bridles with bits were needed for these animals.

From the start, the ranchmen were impressed with their mounts. Slightly larger, and definitely more powerful than the animals they were used to, each horse was responsive to the slightest suggestion of its rider. A touch of the knee and the animal moved to one side or the other; a slight tilt forward caused it to increase the pace and à backward lean caused it to slow or stop. Before long the men were grinning at each other in appreciation of the horses.

Some miles from the ranch one of the men spotted a group of longhorns at the bottom of a sandy draw. Carlos raised his hand as the group reached the top of the ravine.

"Let Armando and the others give you a demonstration," he suggested. "As you've experienced, our reins form a continuous loop from one side of the head gear to the other." The men nodded. "This allows the rider to drop the rein on the horse's neck and guide his mount with knee pressure, leaving both hands free for the rope without dropping reins for the horse to step on." Used to holding two long reins in one hand, some of the men had wondered about the unbroken reins used by the visitors.

"It's a holdover from the days when we trained war horses and buffalo runners; warriors needed to have both hands free…it sometimes meant the difference between life and death," he added pointedly. He gestured and Armando led the other two at a run down the slope, dodging in and out among the brush and cacti scattered about. The longhorns exploded up the other side of the draw and fled across the desert with two of the men in hot pursuit. Each picked an animal and no matter how it ducked and turned, their horses matched the moves and gained ground; within

60 yards both longhorns were neatly roped and on the ground, due to a clever move with the lariat once the loop was tight around their horns.

A large range bull with enormous horns turned around at the top of the draw. As Armando's horse appeared over the edge, the bull charged, head lowered, horns swinging in a deadly arc. The watching men were sure the horse would be impaled, but it gave a great bound to one side avoiding the attack and as the bull passed Armando dropped his big loop over its horns, swung his mount at full speed around the longhorn and yanked its back feet out from under it with the tightened rope.

"Our horses aren't so agile," commented Rodriguez. "We would have lost one in that encounter."

CHAPTER 7
Books

At supper the big hall was abuzz with reports from the riders about their experiences with the range cattle. At one end of the middle table, Ricardo and Bruno were talking so animatedly that Anna had to gently remind them to eat three times! Even Gissy was waving her spoon and pounding the tray on her highchair, wanting to be included in the conversation.

"How was your afternoon?" Carlos asked his son from across the table.

"Good," replied the boy and turned back to Bruno with another comment. Carlos stared at Anna with an upraised eyebrow.

"They had a wonderful time," she explained with a laugh. "When you left, they joined me for a while in the gardens. We pulled some weeds, picked flowers, peppers, and beans. Your son seems to like the garden as much as ours does…although Bruno's attention span is reduced when there's someone else to play with!"

"We have extensive gardens and flowerbeds in the canyon and when he's not riding with me, Ricardo loves to help Rose and the others tend to them."

"Rose?"

"She's the young mother who came to take care of him when my wife died," he answered, a stricken look crossing his face. "She has a little girl almost exactly his age." He quickly changed the subject. "What did they do the rest of the afternoon?"

"For a long time they sat with Christa in the court-yard looking at picture books. Then it was playing with the model train and motor car."

"I heard talk of a powered wagon they call a motor car the last time I was in Santa Fe," mused Carlos.

"There are some beginning to appear in Mexico City," interjected Rodriguez. "Before long, I think they're going to become a way of life." Carlos raised his eyebrows but said nothing; no such thing could make its way through the rugged terrain into his canyon.

"They finally wound up at the stream," Anna continued. "We've diverted water to make a shallow pond and the children love to build forts at the edge and sail their little boats. Both of them fell in, but the water's only this deep." She held her hands about six inches apart.

"It happens all the time in our little irrigation ditches," smiled Carlos. "What did he think about the books? I've seen them in town, but we don't have any at home."

"Christa says he was fascinated. He'd never seen a picture of a giraffe or an elephant." At his blank look, she explained, "Those are animals from across the ocean in Africa." Carlos nodded, but she could see it meant nothing to him.

"Perhaps we could send some books home with you," said Christa from her place across the table.

"I would be very grateful," replied Carlos. "The only lands we know about are in the far north and the far south. Lands in the south of vast mountains, from which the family originally came, and lands in the north of endless snow, visited by my ancestors."

"Didn't you say the family was Aztec?" asked Jorge.

"Yes, but our forefather, Adzul, originally came from the Inca Empire." Christa stared at him in astonishment.

"That's in South America. Your ancestor came all the way north to Mexico?"

'Yes, he was fleeing the conquistadors," he nodded. "Do you know about the Inca?"

"I do," explained the older woman. "I studied history for many years."

"Do you know about great forests to the north of here, oceans with whales, and lands beyond where it's dark all winter and great white bears roam the ice?"

"Yes," she replied. "What you describe sounds like what is now Canada, the Pacific Ocean, and the Arctic."

"Our family has had many adventures in those places," announced Carlos to his astonished listeners, "but we know nothing of these other lands."

Later that evening, as the two boys undressed for their bath, Bruno noticed Ricardo take his shirt off and carefully remove a braided string from around his waist.

"What's that?" he asked.

"It's my sling," replied his guest, dashing toward the bathtub to be first into the wonderful warm water.

"What's a sling?" Bruno wanted to know when both were settled in and watching the little boats bob about.

"It's for throwing rocks. Sometimes I use it for hunting rabbits, but you have to be careful not to scare them away before you get close enough."

"I can throw rocks a long way!" Bruno announced proudly.

"Not as far as a sling," said Ricardo, leaning forward to blow on one of the little sails. "I'll show you tomorrow."

The next morning after breakfast the boys scampered to the edge of the pasture beside the barnyard. Bruno stooped to collect several small rocks from the ground.

"Watch this!" he cried, hurling one as far as he could. The stone flew through the air and landed about 15 yards away.

"Good throw," complimented his companion, selecting a small rock from the little sack tied to his waist. Moving a little to one side, he loaded the sling and gave it three strong revolutions before releasing the missile. It arced slightly upward and landed more than 50 yards ahead. Bruno stared, open-mouthed.

"I want to learn how to do that," he said finally.

CHAPTER 8

Diamondback

"Was that the same hacienda we visited over spring vacation?" asked Sophia. A week had passed and they were on the front porch of their relative's trim white house savoring coffee and a wonderful pineapple-upside-down cake he'd produced.

"The very same," smiled Great Grandfather.

"The description matches what we saw," commented Juan. "The large house is on one side of a stream, with a complex of barns and corrals on the other side. But the pastures are all fenced now."

"Yes," replied his relative. "The days of open range are gone, although the Rodriguez family has more than 100,000 acres of land. Fencing the irrigated areas helps with herd management and keeps the cattle off the grass until fields are hayed."

"We saw a lot of haystacks."

"The desert isn't great for producing feed, so they have to grow it themselves," replied the old man.

"You experienced a bathtub and warm water for the first time," said Sophia. "That must have been quite a change from the canyon."

"Señor Rodriguez and Anna were quite innovative," explained Great Grandfather. "Their ranch in Mexico had been gradually surrounded by the city and they'd been introduced to a lot of conveniences that New Mexicans didn't have yet. They diverted water from the creek into a large wooden water tank buried in a hilltop upstream from the house. Underground pipes fed the house by gravity and a wood-fired boiler supplied hot water."

"Those were modern conveniences," observed Juan.

"By the second time I came to live with them, they had a generator that supplied lights at night and ran a refrigerator," said the old man.

"You lived with them twice?"

"I lived with them once for nearly two years when I was seven and a second time for 18 months when I was twelve," said Great Grandfather. I also visited many times after we settled in the San Luis Valley."

"You and Bruno must have been good friends," said Sophia.

"He was one of my best friends. His grandson is the man you met at the ranch on your spring break."

"Did Bruno ever learn to use the sling?" asked Juan.

"Not immediately…" the old man stared at the front lawn as memories washed over him.

After the sling demonstration, Bruno wanted to know if the throw had been lucky or whether his new friend could actually hit a rabbit on purpose. They returned to the corrals, where Ricardo hung a bit of cloth on one of the posts. After he hit it three times in a row from a distance of 15 yards, not only was Bruno impressed but so were several of the cowhands saddling horses.

"That's an old fashioned weapon," said one of the ranchmen who happened to have Aztec ancestry, "but it can be as deadly as a firearm at close range."

"How does a kid that young get so accurate?" questioned another.

"Seeing how he rides," mused the first, "I'd say he started practicing both very young!" The others nodded as they headed out to look for range cattle.

Bruno insisted Ricardo begin teaching him the sling immediately but when he experienced the usual troubles of a beginner, including banging himself on the back of the head with the loaded pouch, he lost interest. It wasn't until the following day that he began to appreciate the true potential of the weapon.

They had taken their sailboats down to the little pond and were busy watching a gentle breeze blow them across the water. Bruno was walking around the edge, intent on retrieving their tiny craft, when a distinct rattling noise stopped him in his tracks. Well trained in the ways of the desert, the boy didn't move a muscle; not two feet away under a bush was coiled a large Diamondback rattlesnake, which neither of them had noticed. Had Bruno taken another step it would have struck; now, rattles whirring, its head was poised to dart forward at the slightest provocation.

"Don't move," Ricardo's voice came softly across the pond. Lifting his shirt, he removed his sling, loaded it, and started slowly along the water's edge. When he was 18 feet from the snake, he started rotating the weapon rapidly above his head. The snake's eyes flickered at the sound but before it could react the rock struck it full in the head, killing it instantly.

"That rattler was close," said Bruno calmly. "When we are surprised by one, my father usually shoots it with his pistol. But he won't let me have a pistol, so I'd better learn the sling."

When the visitors left the next day, Ricardo presented Bruno with his sling, telling him to practice far away from barns, horses, pigs, chickens, and humans. The cowhand with Aztec ancestors had used a sling in his youth and agreed to help the youngster learn. He promised that by the next time they saw each other Ricardo would be amazed at his friend's prowess.

A year later, Carlos and Ricardo again herded horses to the hacienda, accompanied by Armando. They stayed for three days, during which time the boys were inseparable. They rode, cavorted in the pond, and hunted rabbits with their slings. Bruno had been diligent in practicing but lagged behind his friend in accuracy. He brought home half the number of rabbits as his guest and when Ricardo introduced him to quail, just shook his head.

"I'll be better next time," was all he could say.

But it was books that occupied them the most. Ricardo returned the picture books he had taken home and they were passed to Gissy. Under Christa's teaching, Bruno had started to read. The boy from the canyon was mesmerized by his friend's ability to comprehend the squiggly markings that sometimes filled up whole pages. When Bruno wasn't working his way through a text, Christa would read aloud to them from a storybook.

Sitting under umbrellas in the courtyard, the boys were treated to stories of princes, kings, and adventures in far away lands. Invariably there were pictures and Ricardo feasted his eyes on castles with high towers and flags shown blowing in the wind. His favorite stories usually involved dragons; he never tired of seeing pictures of the great winged creatures with fire coming from their mouths. When it was time to return home, he took one of the storybooks with him just for its dragon renderings.

CHAPTER 9

Tukor

DURING INFREQUENT TRIPS to Santa Fe, Carlos and Ricardo would stay at the house of Carlos' grandfather, Tukor. Perched on a little hill just outside the town, it had sweeping views of the desert to the south. In what was an unusual design for the time, large windows extended almost from floor to ceiling throughout the dwelling, creating a feeling of brightness and light within the entire home. Beautiful dark-wood floors were scattered with colorful throw rugs and the furniture was exquisitely crafted from cedar.

From the time he was a little boy, Ricardo loved the small white carved animals that graced tabletops in every room. They weren't like the horses and desert animals he was familiar with and he would stand for long minutes studying each one, trying to imagine where it lived. The one animal he recognized, however, was bigger than the others and occupied the center of a low table before a couch in the living room. About six inches high, it was a wolf delicately carved out of black wood. The wolf was in the act of springing at a rabbit crouched in front of it. The rabbit, however, was pure white—carved from the same material as all the other figures in the house.

"That's Shadow," his great grandfather would explain each time he found the boy kneeling by the carving. "He's pouncing at an Arctic hare."

"Tell me the story about how you found him," Ricardo would ask.

Side-by-side on the couch, the old man would retell the story to the rapt child. No matter how many times this ritual was repeated, the boy never tired of it, knowing that at the end his relative would invariable say, "Did I ever tell you about the time…" and launch into another wonderful tale. Sometimes more than an hour would go by before the old man would excuse himself to go and stare out a window at two men working in the vegetable garden. From time to time he would open a nearby door and call instructions to them. Ricardo wondered how he could see anything through the thick spectacles with extremely dark lenses he always wore.

"He damaged his eyes years ago in the north," his father had explained. "There was a terrible fight with a bear, after which he became snow blind as he tried to find his way back to the village. He would have died but for Shadow. He finally recovered, but when he returned to the canyon his eyes gradually became so sensitive to light that he had to move to town to be close to the eye doctor. The doctor designed those dark glasses to protect his eyes, so we made the house as light as we could because he hates to be indoors. He supervises the gardeners through the windows, but often he'll go out at night and work in the garden all alone in the moonlight."

During the winter that he became seven, Ricardo and his father were summoned to Tukor's house. After supper, his great grandfather joined the boy and Carlos on the couch by the carved wolf.

"The time has come," he said, pulling on a leather strap around his neck and lifting a circular piece of silver from under his shirt. "I am very old and won't live much longer." He raised a hand as the boy started to protest. "It's all right; I've lived longer than I should, and have had many adventures, but we can't live forever. You are the youngest member of the family and I must pass the medallion on to you. It's been carried by our family for almost 400 years. It possesses a great secret which some day one of us may discover. If it's not to be you, you are to wear it for the rest of your life and pass it to the youngest family member before you die. Do you understand?"

"Yes," said the boy solemnly, staring at the ornament with strange symbols carved on it and a square hole in the middle. "It seems too big for me."

"So it is," laughed the old man. "I was nearly full grown when I received it, but the family history involves tales of young children who've worn it. We'll see. Duck your head," he said, holding out the strap. Ricardo noticed the metal was extremely light as it was hung from his neck.

"Tuck it inside your shirt," said the old man softly. With some difficulty, because of the medallion's size, Ricardo complied. Father and great grandfather leaned forward, staring intently at the boy.

"Now, pull it out again," ordered the old man, even more softly. Confused by the reversal of directions, Ricardo reached for the strap and pulled. From under his shirt emerged the medallion, its diameter shrunk to fit the boy proportionally as it had the man! All the markings were intact and the square hole remained, but the silver piece had shrunk appropriately to the size of the boy.

"How did that happen?" cried the Ricardo.

"We don't know, Son," replied Carlos. "Before your great grandfather, there were a couple of times when the new Wearers were quite young. We didn't know what would happen tonight, but it appears the stories were true." The two men grinned at each other.

"You will also discover that the medallion will protect you," said the older man. "It saved my life more than once."

"Will you tell me about it?" asked Ricardo, putting the medallion back under his shirt.

"Yes. You're going to spend a few weeks here and I'm going to tell you much of the family history. Later, your father can fill in whatever I don't cover; he knows the details as well as I do. He tells me you are already adept with the sling, but he and I are also going to teach you some weaving."

"Weaving?" questioned the boy doubtfully.

"Yes. You'll be astonished at the results."

CHAPTER 10

Longevity

"It SHRANK?" EXCLAIMED JUAN, pulling the medallion from under his shirt and staring at it. "It actually shrank?"

"It actually did," responded Great Grandfather with a smile.

"Why didn't it shrink for me?"

"You were closer to adult size two years ago, not a little kid barely seven years old. I guess it wasn't necessary for you. Besides, it's only happened three times in the family's history," added Great Grandfather.

"That's so cool!" cried Sophia. "Did it change size again?"

"Not noticeably," he said. "Somehow it was always proportionally perfect as I grew. When I became an adult it was the same size it is now."

"So Tukor wound up in Santa Fe," said Juan. "And finally passed the medallion on to you…"

"You're right, Tukor was my great grandfather."

"But…he must have been *really* old by the time you were seven," stated Juan.

"He was close to 125, I think," answered Great Grandfather.

"That's crazy! No one lives to be 125," interjected Sophia.

"It's extremely rare," acknowledged her relative. "But we've never understood all the properties of the medallion, one of which may be to grant the Wearer long life."

"We've talked about this before," said Juan. "You outperform men 25 years younger with your gardening and marketing; you're always taking care of people like Mrs. Martinez. At 102, you're a living example before our very eyes of the power of the medallion!"

"I suppose," mused the old man. "But, as I've said before, the revelations into the past given the two of you may mean we're getting close to discovering its secret. Who knows what will happen after that?" The twins were silent for a few minutes contemplating this statement. Finally, Sophia glanced up with a smile.

"You've got us all stirred up about Tukor's blind-ness. Now will you tell us how it happened and how his story ends?"

"Come back in a week and we'll see," Great Grandfather grinned. "Now be off with you; I've got produce to tend to!"

CHAPTER 11

Shoreline

THE FROZEN RIVERS were like highways through the great forests and mountains, allowing the three dogsleds to travel steadily north. Although it had been many years, Qimmiq and Tikaani had an instinctive ability to find connecting watercourses, which kept them from leaving the frozen waterways to make their way cross country through the dark timber. At night they were treated to incredible displays of colored light: brilliant bands of green, red, gold, and purple bending in great horizontal arcs or shooting vertically into the sky. Tukor had seen distant displays like this from the Makah village, but these extraordinary spectacles dominated the vast reaches overhead.

As weeks passed, daylight hours grew longer and the bitter cold started to abate. The Inuits lengthened daily travel times as the temperature rose, racing against the breakup of river ice. Gradually the mountains receded and the little party left forests for more open terrain. Patches of ground began to emerge from the snow, freed by increasing intensity of the sun. The ice softened on the last river they traveled, but held long enough for them to reach its end one afternoon. Tukor stared: on either side of the waterway were great patches of bare earth from which coarse grass was beginning to show green and here and there a few flowers poked red petals in the air. Directly in front of them, however, was a vast expanse of snow stretching to the horizon. He turned in confusion to Tikaani.

"It's the ocean," explained his friend. "We've reached the shore, but the ice hasn't started to break up yet. When it starts to melt, our people, who winter out there to hunt seals, will come back to the shore to spend the summer."

They made camp on a patch of open ground and for the next few days Tukor and Shadow explored the low range of hills to the south. The man learned to have his sling ready all the time because the great black wolf, running about sniffing the terrain, often startled large white rabbits. These animals were nearly invisible against the snowy background and would hold their position until Shadow was almost on top of them, then race away at high speed with the wolf in hot pursuit. A deadly missile from the sling usually ended the race and Shadow was rewarded with a fine meal. The rabbits were plentiful, however, and by the end of the day Tukor usually returned to camp with enough to feed the humans.

A week after they reached the ocean, Tukor was startled to hear a loud "boom." He and Shadow were on the crest of a hill about a mile from camp and the sound had come from behind them in the direction of the water. He remembered the weapons carried by the white men he'd visited down the coast; the Makah had told him the great ships sometimes appearing near their shores had much larger weapons, which made a loud roar that could be heard for miles. He wondered whether such a ship might have come north and searched the horizon for it, but there was nothing to be seen. The sound came again, and again, and yet again. He hurried toward camp, curious about the noise.

"It's the ice," explained Qimmiq. "It's starting to break up. Soon the ocean will be free and we will be able to fish. The caribou will also come back; their meat is excellent. Our people won't be far away," he added, waving a hand east and west. "It will be a fine summer!"

The excitement to find their people mounted daily with the Inuits and two days later they set out to find them, leaving Tukor to maintain camp. Qimmiq headed west along the coast and Tikaani went east. Each took four dogs packed with food and supplies.

"We'll return when we've found a village," promised Tikaani as he strode away.

But a week went by and neither reappeared. Every day Tukor had to stake out the remaining sled dogs while he and Shadow roamed the hills. They all wanted to go with him but were unruly when turned loose, scaring any game away long before he had a chance to use the sling. They howled mournfully when he left but were only too happy with the food he brought back for them.

During these forays Tukor began to notice the wolf lifting his head and sniffing, staring south toward the distant mountains. He scanned the landscape and could see nothing, but clearly Shadow was picking up a scent blown to them on the wind. A few days later the man saw something move at the far limits of his vision. It was just a speck, but after a minute another speck joined it. Sitting down, Tukor cupped his hands around his eyes and focused all his attention on the distant images. Shadow sat close beside him, mouth open as though grinning: at last his companion had noticed what he already knew to be there. When they finally rose to leave, the man knew that the specks were four legged and brown. The next day the specks were decidedly closer and accompanied by others.

"They're coming our way," said Tukor, one arm around the big wolf as they sat together on a hilltop. "Whatever they are, we'll soon know." Shadow just stared intently at the distant animals.

Two days later the creatures were close enough to be clearly visible. They were smaller than the southern elk he had hunted, and all of them were antlered. In fact, some of the antlers were gigantic: disproportionate to the size of animal carrying them. With bodies of varying shades of brown, most had white on the chest. By now there were many scattered across the landscape and more seemed to be coming. The New Mexican decided to stalk them.

With no horse for speed and no trees for cover, the hunt took several hours. Tukor picked one animal and crept toward it, Shadow at his side. They moved only when the antlered head was lowered to graze, the wolf in perfect synchrony with its master. Tukor had taught Shadow to wait until the sling was released before charging; ordinarily, the quarry was dead before he pounced on it. This time was no different: when the man rose from a few yards away the startled prey dashed off, only to fall with a shattered skull before traveling 40 feet.

As more and more of the antlered animals appeared, hunting became easier and man, dogs, and wolf feasted on fresh meat daily. Along the shore, open water began to appear as the ice broke and melted. Birds materialized in great numbers. Tukor was familiar with some, like bald eagles, hawks, and a variation of owl which spent much of its time on the ground. Others were new to him and fascinating. One was a large bird with an enormous wingspan that soared high in the sky, only to swoop down and gracefully skim the waves; it never landed, just rode the wind currents until it was a distant speck in the sky. Another bird he loved to watch was black, with an odd-shaped red beak, white face, and yellow tufts at the back of its head. It would dive into the water and completely disappear, emerging yards away with a fish in its beak and lift off into the air.

CHAPTER 12
Arctic Wildlife

"Was that some kind of duck?" asked Sophia. "We've seen ducks go underwater on ponds and show up some distance away." Saturday morning on Great Grandfather's front porch was a favorite time for the twins as he relayed the adventures of their ancestors. The delectable baked goods he produced always enhanced it; today it was large, warm, blueberry scones.

"No, it wasn't a duck," replied their relative. "It was a puffin."

"I think I've heard the name somewhere, but I don't remember anything about them," said the girl.

"It's an Arctic bird a bit larger than a pigeon," explained the old man. "It builds a nest by scooping a hole in the dirt. It actually uses its wings under water to chase small fish and can hold more than one in its beak."

"That's cool!" exclaimed Juan. "It sort of flies under water."

"Right. A duck uses its webbed feet, but the puffin uses its wings."

"What was the big bird?" Juan inquired.

"Ahhh…that one is famous in ocean skies around the world: the albatross," said Great Grandfather. "It rarely lands, except to breed and lay eggs on remote islands in the Pacific. It travels thousands of miles, using wind currents to soar and glide. A large albatross will have a wingspan exceeding 10 feet."

"Thousands of miles?" asked Juan incredulously.

"Yes. Old-time sailors claimed the albatross circumnavigated the earth and they may have been right. There's no question that they can cover extremely long distances," said the old man.

"That's incredible! How does it get food?"

"It can snatch fish close to the surface and even dive a short distance into the water. It also eats squid," added Great Grandfather.

"Does it ever rest?" Juan wanted to know.

"If there's no wind to keep it aloft, it lands on the ocean. The problem with resting on the water is that predators, like sharks or Orcas, are always a danger. There's some thought that it actually sleeps while soaring, but of course that's difficult to research."

"What an amazing bird," mused the boy.

"True," responded Great Grandfather. "There are a lot of amazing creatures in nature. Think of the tiny hummingbirds that fly up here from Central and South America every year in the spring…then turn around and fly all the way back in the fall."

"So Tukor saw eagles and hawks in the Arctic?" asked Sophia.

"Bald eagles and Peregrine falcons," answered Great Grandfather. "As you know, eagles build huge nests in the tops of trees near water. They have astounding long-distance vision and are excellent at snatching fish from just under the water's surface. Peregrines cruise the tundra looking for mice or little rodents called lemmings; they dive-bomb their target and stun it, before killing it."

"I didn't realize there was so much wildlife in the Arctic," said Sophia.

"There's lots," replied her relative, "particularly in the summer. But not all disappear in the winter like the caribou. They adapt. The ptarmigan turns white to blend with the snow. A predator that changes color is the arctic fox. In summer its coat is gray or bluish, but it also turns white in the winter. Then there's the musk ox."

"That's the one with long, shaggy, dark hair and horns, right?" said Juan.

"Yes. It's a pretty peaceful animal, until wolves come around," replied Great Grandfather.

"Oh?" Juan's imagination perked up.

"When wolves show up, the herd forms a circle with females and calves inside, males on the perimeter facing out. If a wolf gets too close, one of the males will hook it with those horns, toss it to the ground and stomp it to death."

"That's nasty," exclaimed the boy.

"The wolves go hungry unless they can isolate a single animal from the herd," acknowledged Great Grandfather.

CHAPTER 13

Discovery

TUKOR WAS BUSY FASHIONING a crude framework
from wood he'd scrounged off the tundra. It was to be
a drying rack for the caribou skin he'd been curing.
Hours of rubbing the animal's brains into the underside
of the hide had made it soft and pliable; now he wanted
to let the thick outside hair dry in the sun. More than
two weeks had passed since the Inuits went searching
for their people.

A shout caused him to look up: Tikaani was
approaching along the shore, his pack-dogs already
racing ahead to greet their friends at camp. Shadow
bounded up to meet them, fur raised along his back,
but when they uniformly groveled in submission he

merely sniffed noses and returned to his spot by the rack.

"Did you find them?" asked Tukor, but he could tell by the other's face that he had not.

"I went for many miles along the coast," answered the Inuit, "but there was no evidence of people. I found the remains of one village, but it was very old." He called the dogs and began to remove their packs.

"There's been no sign of Qimmiq," said Tukor. "Perhaps he found a village and stayed to visit."

"I think we should follow him," replied Tikaani. "There are more likely to be people to the west and we can at least shorten the distance between us. I see the caribou have returned," he added, nodding at the skin. "Did you have any trouble finding them?"

"No, I think they found me," laughed the man from the canyon. "One day they just started to appear."

"They go south in winter," acknowledged Tikaani. "But I've seen them in the distance on my way back. Their hide makes warm clothing." He nodded with approval at the skin draped on the rack.

"There's more open water every day," noted Tukor. "You must have seen the seals and walrus on the rocks as you came by."

"Yes, and when we find my people, we'll hunt both walrus and seals from boats."

"Just like the Makah," replied his friend.

"No, these will be little boats, just for one person. We call them 'qajaq.'"

"Who does the harpooning?" asked Tukor in confusion.

"The hunter in the boat, of course," stated Tikaani. "You'll see. We have bigger boats for fishing and hunting whales, called 'umiaq,' but seals and even walrus can be hunted from the qajaq."

The next day they hauled the three sleds to a little rise and tipped them up against each other so they could be easily seen from shore. The dogs were packed with meat and supplies and the two men set off in the direction Qimmiq had taken. Four days later, as they were about to break camp, Shadow abruptly walked to the edge of the water and stared west into the breeze.

"He smells something," said Tukor, looking down the coast. A moment or two later a dot appeared on the water beside a point of land, half a mile away.

"It's Qimmiq," announced Tikaani.

"How do you know?"

"The boat is very small and riding high in the water, which means it's carrying little except the man. It has to be Qimmiq because anyone else would be carrying a lot of gear. He's coming back by boat because it's much faster than traveling on foot," replied the Inuit. "He must have gone a long way." In a few minutes they could see that it was indeed a man in a tiny boat. He had a long paddle, with blades on both ends, which he dipped into the water on one side of the craft and then the other, approaching at a speed that startled the New Mexican.

"Ho!" cried Qimmiq as he reached them and beached the boat. "I've found the People!"

CHAPTER 14
Inuit Village

"THERE WAS NOTHING TO the east," explained Tikaani. "So we decided to follow you."

"The villages are in the west this year," said his father. "The water opened early and the hunting and fishing is good."

"How much farther?"

"Six more days walking. Fewer by boat," answered the older man. "I'll go back and tell them you're coming. They've already put up a tent for us." An hour later, refreshed by a caribou steak, he set out in his little boat.

"What a difference horses would make now," Tukor exclaimed as they followed on foot. But they pushed the pace and reached the village in the middle of the fifth day. It consisted of 25 low, skin covered structures scattered on a grassy area along the beach. A number of tiny one-man boats, like the one Qimmiq had used, were drawn up on the shore. Barking dogs rushed out to meet them and there was the usual commotion as the dominant male challenged Shadow. A brief but savage fight sent the big husky slinking away with a torn shoulder. Once the wolf had strutted among the rest of the pack, receiving their obeisance, he returned to Tukor's side and paid no further attention to the dogs.

Children crowded around to stare at the strangers. They gave the big wolf a wide berth until Tukor picked up a toddler and let her rub Shadow's head. As with the Makah, once the children were reassured about the animal they accepted him like another dog. Tikaani squatted down and began to ply some of the kids with questions and in minutes was surrounded by a great flock of children vying for his attention. It was obvious that he was delighted to be back among his people after so many years.

"You walked faster than I," exclaimed Qimmiq, approaching with a wide grin.

"Tikaani has been away from your people for too long," laughed Tukor. "He wouldn't let me stop to rest." Leaving the younger Inuit with the kids, they strolled to a skin-covered dwelling at the edge of the village.

"There's not enough wood for poles like the people on the Plains have," said the one-eyed trader. "So we use whalebones, limbs from bushes, even dogsleds, to support our summer dwellings. In winter most houses are made from snow." Tukor nodded, remembering the half-walls Qimmiq and Tikaani had erected as wind protection on their journey north. Their new home was spacious enough for the three of them, although much lower than a teepee.

A few hours later three large boats appeared off shore, accompanied by several qajaq. The crews of the big boats included men and women who, upon landing, began to unload a great catch of fish into the waiting hands of the crowd on shore.

"Most of these will be dried for use in the winter," said Tikaani as they carried armloads of fish to several women wielding strange, oval-shaped knives to slice them open for cleaning. The blade was shaped like a quarter moon, with the handle sticking up between the "horns" of the moon and the sharp edge along the "crescent" of the moon.

"What is that?" asked Tukor. "I've never seen a knife like that."

"It's an 'ulu,'" replied his friend. "My people have always used them, although I didn't see them among the tribes in the south."

"Nor I," agreed the New Mexican. He was amazed at the efficiency with which the women wielded the odd looking tool.

That night the village gathered for a feast to welcome the newcomers. Their language was similar enough to that of the Makah that Tukor could make himself understood; he found them friendly, curious about the wolf, and fascinated by his background. They could relate to a season of warmer weather, but a land where there was no ocean or snow was almost incomprehensible. Were it not for Tikaani coming to his rescue and confirming what the New Mexican said, the villagers would have thought the stranger a little crazy.

CHAPTER 15

Hunting

SUMMER PASSED QUICKLY. Almost every day some of the men were out in their qajaqs, or kayaks, hunting seals that frequented rocky islands close to shore. The animals were difficult to stalk, and handling both harpoon and paddle wasn't easy, but there were countless numbers of them within easy reach of the village and the hunters were highly skilled. The first time Tukor observed one of the kayaks roll over, he was aghast, knowing how cold the water was: the qajaq was a great distance from shore and the paddler would freeze to death before he could swim in. He also knew that most of the Inuit didn't know how to swim. Therefore, he was astonished to see the kayak right itself almost instantly and the hunter continue on his way toward the prey. When he questioned Qimmiq, the old man smiled.

"The qajaq can tip over quite easily," he explained. "But each man knows how to use his paddle and body to quickly bring it upright and continue hunting. He must learn this skill before venturing out onto the ocean," he added unnecessarily.

"But why doesn't the boat fill with water and sink?" asked Tukor.

"The seal-skins covering the kayak are sewn together in such a way that no water can get in," answered the Inuit, "and each boat is customized to the size of its owner, so that he fits tightly. The lower part of his seal-skin coat is laced over the opening around his waist so that no water can enter when the boat tips over." Tukor stared at the old man in amazement.

"It's been the way of our people for time out of memory," said the one-eyed trader, shrugging his shoulders. "It's been many years, but I used to be the best seal hunter in my village." He grinned. "Next summer my son and I will have our own qajaqs and I'll have to show him a thing or two. He was just a boy when he was captured and had never hunted on the ocean."

There were two rivers emptying into the sea not far from the village and sometimes the people would take nets in the larger boats to fish the confluence of river and ocean. At other times they would trek across the tundra and camp for a few days upstream while they hunted fish with bows or spears. As Tikaani had described, almost all the fish were dried and stored as the primary food source for the dogs when winter set in. Caribou, ptarmigan, berries, and certain green plants supplied men, women, and children with food during the brief summer.

Tukor's skill with the sling was greatly admired by the Inuit. They were adept with bow and arrow, but sometimes had to trail wounded caribou for long distances. The New Mexican's headshots dropped the animal almost in its tracks every time. They did use a form of bolo to bring down flying birds: several strands of rawhide weighted at the ends and attached to a central core. The device was thrown at a passing bird to entangle its wings, causing it to fall. The problem was that only a few birds in a flock could be struck before the rest had flown away.

The visitor from the south, however, would sneak up on a group of feeding ptarmigan. With deadly accuracy, he would kill one after another with small rocks to the head while the remaining flock went on pecking at the ground, oblivious to the dead birds. Such performances resulted in both men and women wanting to try the sling. Tukor wisely separated the participants from onlookers; in the evenings the novices showed their bumps and bruises to the amusement of all.

The man from the desert was intrigued by another feature of the far north: during the summer there was practically no night, only a couple of hours of what he would call dusk. The villagers would sleep when they were tired, but at virtually all times some people were up and about, engaged in various activities. As the days lengthened he was a bit disoriented over the lack of darkness, but he soon fell into the Inuit routine. He knew from the trip north with his friends that the coming winter would bring nearly complete dark.

Sure enough, before long the leaves on bushes started to turn orange, the air took on a chill, and a semblance of night began to return. The caribou started to drift away and the hunters were out stalking them every daylight hour. The meat was dried and stored, skins cured and prepared to make heavy winter clothing. The Inuit people had learned centuries before that caribou hair is hollow and, worn close to the skin, creates a life-saving insulating layer due to warm air trapped in and around each strand of hair.

"Your presence has been a great help," said Tikaani, as he and Tukor returned to the village after searching for hours and finding no caribou; even Shadow's keen nose had failed to pick up the scent of lingering prey. "Both the wolf's ability to smell distant caribou, and the accuracy of your sling, have increased our success. The people have told me we nearly doubled the amount of meat they collected last year."

"I fear our assistance is coming to an end," replied his friend. "Rocks aren't much good against seals when they are mostly underwater."

"Not in the water," agreed the Inuit. "But sometimes the seals do get out on the ice close to open water. Shadow will smell them and your weapon might work if the straps don't get frozen"

"I can keep it inside my clothing until it's time to throw," said the New Mexican.

"We'll see," answered Tikaani. "You remember how cold it was coming up the frozen rivers last winter? It's much worse out on the ice in the wind." Three weeks later the first snow fell, covering the ground with 18 inches of white. When Tukor and the others emerged from their tent, it was bitterly cold and the pale sun only a few degrees above the horizon. Winter was on the way.

CHAPTER 16

Separation

In the days that followed, the Inuits set about storing most of the kayaks and retrieving sleds they'd put away for the summer. Rock storage pits were opened and three great piles of dried fish and meat created, each allocated to a group of 15 to 20 people.

"The winter is too harsh to support all these people in the same place," explained Qimmiq. "We divide into small groups and come back together for the summer." Tukor nodded. As large as each food pile was, he knew it wouldn't last each little community very long.

"We're joining Yutu," said Tikaani. "He has 13 people but only three hunters beside himself." The New Mexican knew the man to be fearless, taking his kayak far out in the ocean in search of seals. He had white scars across his left cheek and jaw, the result of a bear attack in his youth, and the source of his name, "Claw."

The three men had fashioned a new sled during the summer and now they loaded it with food, packing their extra sled dogs with clothing and equipment for the months ahead. Yutu's group was heading east and the newcomers, upon reaching their original campsite, would retrieve the sleds they'd used to come north.

For the first week after leaving the village, Yutu's little band made good time traveling along the shore. The weather warmed slightly and the dogs were able to pull the sleds easily. Two of the four women carried infants on their backs under specially designed parkas with extra room inside. The other three children were dressed as miniature versions of adults in seal skin parkas, pants, boots and mittens. They walked along in the tracks made by the sleds, little brown faces edged by fur on the hoods of their parkas.

Tukor had learned about this particular kind of fur early in the summer. He had been stalking caribou when Shadow gave a menacing growl. Years of training normally kept the wolf creeping silently beside him, but this sound signaled danger. Glancing at his companion, the hunter saw hackles raised along the entire length of his back; Shadow was staring off to his left. About 10 yards away was a brown animal the size of a small husky. It had short legs, a wide tan stripe on its side extending to the chest, and a short tail. It looked like a little bear and was standing on what appeared to be a caribou carcass, staring at them with bared teeth.

Tukor knew exactly what the animal was and how it behaved, although he had rarely encountered one, and he immediately stood, sling spinning. Sure enough, it charged with no warning. It was a large wolverine, utterly fearless, armed with vicious claws and teeth capable of killing animals twice its size. As quickly as he reacted, the man couldn't put killing power in his weapon before the animal reached him, but a black blur intercepted it as Shadow intervened. The wolf came in low, seeking to rip the wolverine's neck, but this was no sled dog. The animal spun out of the way and slashed the wolf's shoulder open with one swipe of a claw. The wolf's momentum carried it past the wolverine, which spun to face a new attack...the last move it ever made, as a rock from the now fully powered sling smashed into its skull.

"No caribou today, but we killed a wolverine," Tukor had announced as he dropped the dead animal in front of their tent.

"The mothers will be grateful to you," replied Qimmiq. "And so will I, if you can get another. In fact, you and Tikaani will both be grateful this winter."

"I'm sure we'll run into another one before the summer is over," said Tukor. "But why hunt these smelly carrion eaters?"

"They do smell," acknowledged the older man, "but we prize the fur as outer lining for the hood of a parka. Do you remember when the fur around our hoods froze on some of the colder days last winter?"

"Yes, because of the moist air from our mouths and noses," said the New Mexican, remembering the uncomfortable clusters of ice collecting around his face.

"That was mostly rabbit hair," explained Qimmiq. "The wolverine has an oily fur, which won't freeze in the coldest weather. We value it highly for hoods on parkas."

"In that case, I'll spend some time hunting wolverines," said Tukor. True to his word, he killed enough of the bad tempered predators by the end of the summer to supply all the fur the villagers needed. Now, as the temperature steadily dropped, he observed the benefits first hand: his breathing moistened the fur around his mouth, but it never froze.

Some miles up the coast from where Tukor and the two Inuits had camped the previous spring, a hilly promontory jutted into the ocean. At its tip were clusters of enormous boulders extending well out into the water: ideal habitat for countless seals in the summer. Slightly inland along the base of the hill, Yutu's little group came on a cluster of circular stone walls, each about four feet high, with dirt piled against the outsides. Each wall had a break in it facing a slight downhill slope.

"This will be our winter camp," explained Qimmiq, as everyone set to work unpacking sleds. In short order, snow was swept out of the structures and skins stretched over them to create four dwellings. The entrance to each was secured with a heavy flap and more skins spread on the dirt floor for insulation from the cold ground. Tukor was amazed at the size of their new homes: each could easily accommodate ten people, more if necessary.

The rock walls, protected by a covering of dirt and snow on the outside, provided a strong barrier to the wind, leaving the skin roof as the weakest link. This was corrected after the next big storm brought 20 more inches of snow. Blocks of snow were cut from drifts and fitted together in a dome shape over each dwelling. The inside of the dome quickly glazed over from the warm air, while the outside surface became hard as rock, due to the intense cold. The combination provided effective protection against both wind and cold.

Another feature added to each hut was a snow tunnel extending from the entrance for about 20 feet down the hill. It was big enough to crawl through and made a dramatic difference to the dwelling's comfort.

The only heat inside, other than that from the human bodies, came from a small stone bowl filled with seal oil. In it floated a lighted wick. Before they made the tunnel, the skin over the entrance was blown about by the wind and the inside temperature was nearly the same as that outside. After the tunnel, the structure warmed to the point where very little clothing was needed inside.

"It has to do with the air," Qimmiq explained to the bewildered New Mexican. "The tunnel goes down and the cold air follows it; the warm air stays up inside. The Inuit always try to build a snow house on a high spot."

The improvements came not a moment too soon because a violent storm blew in shortly thereafter. The wind brought snow as fine as dust, making visibility virtually impossible. When people had to venture out for chunks of frozen meat a rope was tied to their waists with someone in the tunnel ready to haul them back if the fine snow clogged their breathing passages and they collapsed. The storm continued for more than a week, accompanied by bitter cold; when it abated the little band was surrounded by a great world of white. Gone was the open water: the dim light of day revealed a bleached, formless plain stretching from horizon to shore. The surface of the ocean had frozen.

CHAPTER 17

Bitter Cold

"That's hard to imagine, sitting here in the sun," said Sophia, gesturing at the colorful flower pots on the porch and immaculate lawn out front. Another week had gone by and only crumbs remained from the apple-cinnamon muffins Great Grandfather had produced when the twins arrived.

"The Arctic in winter is a different world," acknowledged the storyteller.

"Our winters can be bad," exclaimed Juan. "But snow that can choke you to death? Cold that freezes the entire ocean? A hut with only a primitive lamp for heat? And the darkness!" He shook his head. "Sooner or later, no matter how big the storm, we get blue sky and sun."

"That's our frame of reference," agreed Great Grandfather. "But don't forget, for the Inuit such winters were all they knew. For Tukor it was different: he realized someday he'd be home again, just like people today leave warm climates, go to the Arctic or the Antarctic and return."

"How did they cook on that lamp?" Juan wanted to know.

"They didn't," answered the old man. "They ate everything raw."

"Yuck," grimaced the boy.

"And the diet was mostly blubber and fat in the winter," grinned his relative. Juan made another face. "It was vital though," added Great Grandfather, "as a source of heat and energy for their bodies."

"What do you suppose the temperature was?" asked Sophia.

"Anywhere from minus 30 to minus 50 degrees or more, I'd guess," replied the storyteller. "Such temperatures were routinely reported by explorers a century or more ago."

"What about clothing?"

"Layering was critical, just like today, but from different materials of course. We've talked about sealskin boots, pants, mittens, and parkas. The fur was always to the inside, to provide little spaces to trap warm air.

Caribou fur was highly valued for inner garments. There were also feather shirts."

"Shirts made of feathers?" Sophia raised her eyebrows.

"Not flight feathers from the wings, like the ones we usually think of," chuckled Great Grandfather. "They were made from the small body feathers of birds the hunters brought in. The Inuit women would collect them until they had enough to cleverly sew them together as a shirt. Worn next to the skin, the garments were prized for the warmth they provided. It was the same principle as down clothing we use today."

"How did they discover that?" mused Sophia. "It's amazing."

"Not really," replied her relative. "Human ingenuity is not isolated to contemporary times. The ancients had a great deal of knowledge about many things, much of which has been lost to modern people."

"What about polar bears?" Juan asked, anticipating the confrontation Great Grandfather had mentioned.

"Polar bears are incredible animals," said Great Grandfather. "They spend much of their time on the Arctic ice, rarely going to land. The males can weigh half a ton and they're utterly fearless. Their prey consists primarily of seals; in the winter they hunt them at breathing holes in the ice, just like humans.

"The bears have fur on the bottoms of their feet which gives them traction on the ice. Their front feet are slightly webbed and they are incredible swimmers, capable of crossing vast stretches of open water for days at a time. As you know, their fur is white, but their skin is black. White fur is perfect for camouflage and black skin great for absorbing the sun.

"Among all the carnivores, the polar bear is the only one that will stalk humans for food. Other animals become man-eaters, but only because injury has cost them the ability to bring down their natural prey."

"How did Tukor get attacked?" asked Juan.

"That will have to wait till next week," said the old man as he rose and headed for the front door. "I've got vegetable customers coming in a few minutes."

CHAPTER 18

Seal Stalking

THE STORMS WERE BITTER that year and Yutu's hunters had to travel far out on the ice to find seals. The hunters usually went out in parties of two, to cover more territory, but often returned empty handed. They were further hampered by an unrelenting succession of storms, during which travel was virtually impossible. Two months after they had arrived at the promontory, Yutu made the decision to move the entire band onto the ice pack; their supply of food was dangerously low and the hunting range had to be extended. Moving the village out on the ice would create a base camp, allowing hunters to range much further toward fringes of open water where seals were more likely to be.

Supplies were loaded onto sleds and the little group set out. It was rough going because the ocean, constantly moving under the ice, thrust the frozen surface upward in places, creating jagged hills across the route. Some of these ridges were more than 20 feet high and the heavy sleds had to be manhandled up one side and down the other. It was exhausting work for both dogs and humans. Day after day they moved forward, until the coastal hills were lost to sight and they were surrounded by a vast expanse of white.

Finally, on a slightly elevated area, igloos were constructed. Each had an approach tunnel facing away from the prevailing wind and with the slightest downward angle. The structures were much smaller than the ones on the promontory but just as efficient; Tukor never failed to be amazed at the warmth inside.

The prospects for hunting were much improved by being a day's travel from open water, more conducive for the air-breathing seals than the thick ice pack. Food for the dogs was nearly gone; so only four hunters went out at a time, in pairs, to conserve energy. The strategy was simple: spot seals up on the ice and stalk them, or find a breathing hole and wait by it for one of the animals to poke its head out for air. The first expedition came back two days later with one seal, enough to feed everyone a meal but not nearly what 13 people and dogs needed.

Tukor and Qimmiq paired up for the second hunt. They set out with a sled pulled by six dogs and headed slightly west in the dusk-like winter conditions. Nine hours later, a dark band stretched across the vista in front of them.

"Open water," said the Inuit. "Watch for seals at the edges." Tukor nodded, a hand on Shadow's back to keep the big animal close beside him. Then he saw them: a cluster of black dots nearly a quarter mile ahead to the right.

"There," he said, but Qimmiq had already brought the sled to a stop.

"We'll stake out the dogs and leave the sled," announced the older man. "I'm not sure about the sling, but bring your bow. There's an ice hill not far from them which will give us some cover, but we'll have to circle back and around until we can get behind it. From there we'll crawl the last 100 yards."

Moving slowly, the men unharnessed the dogs and staked them well apart from one another to avoid fights; the exhausted animals immediately dug little holes, curled up in them and went to sleep. Qimmiq rummaged around in the supplies piled on the sled and pulled out a rectangular piece of fur, made from two Arctic fox skins sewn together, and two sticks about 24 inches long. Tucking the articles into his parka, he motioned for Tukor to follow him back along their trail.

When the black specks were nearly invisible, the two men made a wide circle until the distant ridge was between them and the seals. Hidden from the animals' sight, they strode rapidly forward until they reached the ten-foot-high hill. Peering cautiously over the top, they observed eight seals scattered about the ice within 15 feet of the water. As Qimmiq had noted, there was no cover for 100 yards between the animals and the ridge.

"There's a crack in the ridge just to our left," whispered the Inuit. "We'll crawl through it and onto the ice." Tukor nodded, wondering how they were going to avoid alarming the seals. "What about the wolf?" murmured Qimmiq.

"He'll crawl between us," replied Tukor, ignoring the question in the Inuit's eyes. Years of hunting together had taught the animal to stay beside the man until released. The Inuit shrugged and headed for the crack.

Just before they emerged into full view of the seals, Qimmiq withdrew the white fox skins from his parka. He put the end of one stick into a cleverly designed sleeve on the inside of the skin at one corner and inserted the other stick into a similar sleeve at the opposite corner. He held one stick in his left hand and handed the other to Tukor, who nodded his head in admiration. It was a camouflage device. The skin with its white fur on the outside, measuring a little more than three feet wide and two feet high, blended perfectly with the snow and created a "blind" for them to crawl behind. By lifting it slightly, they could peek from underneath and observe their prey.

As the men moved forward on their bellies, the seals seemed to take little notice. If one raised its head to stare, the hunters would stop until it lowered its head to the ice. In this manner the men and wolf progressed until they were 25 yards from the nearest animal.

From a prone position Tukor couldn't use the sling, so Qimmiq held the blind while he carefully removed and strung his bow. When an arrow was notched he nodded at the older man. The Inuit gradually raised the blind until there was enough room to shoot from underneath. At the last instant the seal jerked its head up, but it was too late: an arrow buried itself deep in its neck. The animal was tough, however, and frantically scrabbled across the ice after the others as they fled for the ocean. It might have reached the water, but a black body hurtled forward with a snarl to sink teeth into it and hold it back. The seal thrashed around violently but couldn't escape the fangs clamped on it and the fight was soon over.

"I see why you hunt with the wolf!" exclaimed the Inuit. "The arrow wouldn't have stopped the seal from reaching water. The dead body might have floated up, but without a boat it would be difficult to retrieve."

The two hungry men shared the raw, hot, nutritious liver before Tukor went to get sled and dogs while Qimmiq carved out some meat. After feeding their animals, they continued but saw no further seals. Moving away from the open water they searched the ice pack until, several hours later, Qimmiq found what they were looking for: a spot about five feet across where the ice was less than an inch thick.

"It's a breathing hole," he said as they quickly moved sled and dogs behind a small snowdrift nearby. He pulled a harpoon and a long length of braided rope from the sled. "This may take some time, because it hasn't been used for a while, but seals should come back." In a few minutes both men were sitting cross-legged at the edge of the thin ice, Shadow curled in a ball behind Tukor.

The harpoon lay on the snow beside Qimmiq. It was comprised of a four-foot wooden shaft, one end of which had been hollowed out to hold an eight-inch ivory point shaped like half of a large arrowhead. One end of the rope, neatly coiled beside the Inuit, was attached to a hole in the butt end of the ivory blade.

The hunters sat motionless for several hours, only their eyes moving occasionally to check the surrounding area. Their competition for seals was the polar bear: huge, fearless, and just as likely to eat them as seals. The dogs would alert them to a bear's approach, but the big animals could move swiftly and might be on them before they could react.

Suddenly a shadow shot past under the thin section of ice.

"Seal," breathed Qimmiq. "It's studying the hole." The animal passed by twice more, cautious that danger might lurk above. On the next swing, it sharply rapped the ice with its nose, breaking the surface and creating open water.

A minute later, with no warning the seal's head came up for a breath.

Despite hours of immobility in the bitter cold, Qimmiq's arm moved like a striking snake as he drove the harpoon into the animal's neck. The seal instantly dove, pulling the ivory head out of the shaft. Handing the wood to Tukor, the Inuit grasped the rope with both mittens as it uncoiled into the icy darkness after the frantic seal. Gradually, he applied pressure with his hands until he was able bring the animal to a stop.

"It will never come back to the surface," he said, "and will drown shortly if the wound doesn't kill it." Sure enough, some minutes later the line went slack and they hauled the dead seal back to the surface and onto the ice.

"We won't cut it open," announced the Inuit. "The blood might attract a bear and another seal may come to this breathing hole." His prediction came true two hours later when another animal poked its head up to breathe.

"The meat will be welcome at the village," remarked Tukor as they started for home.

CHAPTER 19

Starvation

Slowly but surely the sun began to stay above the horizon for longer periods each day and the nights grew shorter. The storms abated, but bitter cold persisted and the seals, which the village had come so far to hunt, began to disappear. The older men had no explanation and hunters were forced to range far and wide in search of prey. Once again the hunters were limited to two pairs, leaving dogs for the unused sleds at the village. One day this strategy proved useful as a polar bear was spotted stalking the igloos.

Upon catching the bear's smell, the sled dogs set up such a commotion of howls and barking that it was hard for people to hear one another. The dogs, hurriedly released from their stakes, took off in a mad dash toward the bear. The two hunters who had remained in the village followed close behind, arrows notched in their bows. Racing madly around the bear, the huskies kept just out of reach as the big white animal turned one way and then another in an attempt to catch one of them. In a short time, the fracas was over as well placed arrows brought down the bear.

When the other hunters returned empty handed a few days later, there was still meat to feed them and their dogs, but one bear isn't sufficient to keep 16 people and their dogs alive for very long and the Inuit never ceased their search for game. Three weeks later another marauding bear was killed at the village, but it was small and the meat didn't last long. By now, adults were beginning to weaken since most of the food was given to the children. Hunting was now carried on solely by the two strongest men, usually Tukor and Tikaani, each heading in a different direction. Finally, the situation became so desperate that the two friends agreed not to return without food…even if it cost their lives.

Four days out and far to the west, the New Mexican was stumbling behind his severely weakened dogs when he spotted a small breathing hole that wasn't iced over: it had been used recently. He croaked commands for the dogs to drag the sled a short distance away and left them in the harness, the exhausted animals simply collapsing where they were. Moving like a drunken man, he pulled harpoon and rope from the sled and staggered to the side of the hole.

Despite his weakened condition, Tukor focused carefully on his preparations: making sure the ivory point was properly inserted in the end of the shaft and coiling the rope carefully at his side. Any mistake could result in the loss of a seal and perhaps his own death. This activity was made awkward by a strip of wood worn across his eyes to protect them from the brilliant reflection of the sun on the snow. Narrow slits in the wood kept the glare off his pupils, but restricted his vision; nevertheless, he left the wood in place for safety, holding the harpoon up to his eyes until satisfied it was correctly assembled. As he sat down, he felt the familiar pressure of Shadow against his back. The wolf had adopted this position months earlier when Tukor first frequented the breathing holes.

Settled at the side of the hole, the New Mexican was attacked by an overwhelming drowsiness. He hadn't eaten for three days; the last food had gone to the dogs and Shadow. The entire winter had been harsh and food scarce. He and the rest of the village were starving to death, and he had used his last reserves of strength getting to the watering hole. Gradually his head slumped lower on his chest and he started to topple over as he lost consciousness.

Suddenly, his body straightened when an electric shock from the medallion coursed through him as though he'd been struck by lightning. In an instant he was wide awake, the skin on his chest literally pulsing with heat. Under the hood, the hair on his head tingled as though someone had pulled on it and he could feel the hair on his arms sticking up. Eyes that had been impossible to keep open were sharply focused on the surroundings through the slits in the wood covering them. Turning his head slowly, he searched for danger but the pressure of the wolf at his back reassured him that nothing was amiss.

Glancing at the water in front of him, Tukor saw a flash of movement as a seal darted past. He gripped the wood shaft of the harpoon, his mind now clear and alert. Minutes went by before a sleek head burst above the surface and the harpoon was rammed home with full force.

Tossing the shaft to the ice, he concentrated on trying to slow the rope flying through his mittens. But, despite the mental clarity, all his strength had gone to driving the harpoon into the seal's neck and he couldn't control its dive. Glancing at the disappearing coils, he realized the rope might be pulled through his hands and into the depths. In a desperate move, he flung the end of the rope around his waist and looped it over one hand just as the last coil disappeared. The violent jerk on his body almost pulled him into the water, but he dug his heels into the snow and leaned back against the pressure. The seal was powerful and for a moment the New Mexican thought he was going to be pulled after it, but the harpoon thrust had been true and the animal began to weaken. A short while later he dragged it onto the ice.

After cutting great chunks of meat for the dogs and Shadow, Tukor gorged on the liver and heart and returned to his spot by the breathing hole. In less than four hours he killed three more seals, the maximum number he could take on the sled. After a short nap, he fed the dogs, Shadow, and himself, loaded the sled and started for home.

Although the meat had greatly refreshed man and dogs, they were still weak from the starvation existence of past weeks and going was slow with the heavy load. Tukor tried to help the huskies by pushing the sled from behind, but he was only good for an hour at a time before his strength ran out and he had to simply trudge along, one hand resting loosely on the wood handle. Fortunately, the weather remained clear and their tracks coming from the village were easy to follow in the brilliant sunlight. As they made their way through the vast panorama of shimmering white, the New Mexican gradually fell into a mindless reverie, rousing himself only to feed the dogs and consume the meat he kept for himself inside his parka to prevent to prevent it from freezing.

CHAPTER 20
Polar Bear

On the third day, more than halfway home, burning heat from the medallion and the wolf's ferocious growl broke his trance. All at once the huskies set up a furious din of barking and stopped in their tracks. Now fully alert, Tukor swung around to stare at his back trail. Less than a hundred yards away, a large polar bear was loping purposefully toward them! It must have smelled the remaining meat from the first seal, stacked on top of the load.

Moving quickly, the man loosed the dogs from their harnesses. That action probably saved his life because the six dogs went for the bear in a howling pack, forcing it to slow and face them. The huskies raced around it snarling and yipping, but keeping their distance. Finally, one ventured too close and was caught by a lightning-quick swipe of a great paw. The husky, nearly cut in two, flew through the air to land in an inert mass yards away. The other dogs, although still barking and snarling, backed off and the bear resumed its advance.

Tukor had been frantically trying to reach his bow and arrows, but they were under the frozen seals, pinned to the sled. Glancing over his shoulder, he saw the bear approaching and knew he didn't have time to retrieve them. The harpoon, lashed on top of the load, was the only weapon available. He grabbed it and turned to face the massive animal. It paused and stood up on its hind legs, fully nine feet tall. Suddenly Shadow darted in and slashed one of the legs with his teeth. A bright streak of red appeared on the white fur and the bear gave a great snarl, dropping to all fours and striking at the wolf, but the black body was already out of reach.

Encouraged, the five dogs closed in again, yapping and growling. Shadow remained quiet, crouched low to the ground. When one of the dogs got too close, the bear hooked it in with a massive paw and, while it was distracted, the wolf attacked again from the rear, tearing at the animal's hamstring. The bear's fur was thick enough to keep those teeth from severing the vital tendon, but another wound was opened and blood poured out. Whirling from the body of the dog, the bear lunged for the wolf but Shadow was too quick and skipped away.

In the meantime, Tukor had dropped mittens to fumble in his clothing. His garments were bulky and in frustration, he threw back his hood and flipped off the piece of wood protecting his eyes. Squinting in the sun's brilliance, he finally pulled his sling free and retrieved a rock from the pouch under his feather shirt.

The dogs and wolf were keeping the bear occupied 10 yards from the sled, but the predator was intent on getting to the seals and kept pressing closer. Tukor circled behind it, sling whirling, and gave a mighty shout. The bear turned, roared, and charged. In the split second the animal's mouth was open to roar, Tukor's rock hurtled into it and broke the bear's jaw; simultaneously, Shadow came in from behind and this time his teeth found their mark, severing the hamstring. But the vitality of the 1,000-pound animal was astounding and it kept coming for the man on three legs, blood pouring from its now slack-jawed mouth.

There was no time to reload the sling and Tukor ran for the sled. The four dogs and Shadow were viciously assaulting the bear's hindquarters, but it ignored them, focused on the man. Backed against the sled, the New Mexican gripped the harpoon in two hands and as the bear reached him, he stepped forward and rammed the harpoon underhanded into the gaping jaws, through the roof of the mouth, piercing the bear's skull. The blow was enough to kill the bear, but as it died it delivered a tremendous swipe of its paw, breaking two of Tukor's ribs and hurling him through the air.

A wet nose and whimpering brought the man back to consciousness: Shadow stood over him, black head mercifully blotting out the sun. Tukor tried to rise, but excruciating pain radiating through his chest forced him back. Memory of the fight returned and he rolled his head toward the sled. Beside it the four huskies were still worrying the body of the polar bear.

"I think you saved us, old friend," he said weakly to the wolf, raising one hand to its face. "The bear would have had me but for your attacks. Now we've got to get this meat to the children in the village." After many minutes he turned over on his stomach and got to all fours, nearly passing out from the pain. Crawling to the sled, he used it to pull himself upright.

"Got to have mittens," he mumbled, spotting them on the snow nearby. He went to one knee, keeping his upper body as straight as possible to diminish the intense pain caused by bending. Moving slowly, he cut two of the seals free and let the bodies fall to the snow: the remaining four dogs couldn't pull the full load and he was going to have to ride some of the time. He never remembered how he harnessed the dogs, but finally the sled was moving, the man balanced on the backs of the runners, barely able to grip the handles.

The only thing that kept him going was the idea that children in the village would starve to death without the food he was bringing.

An hour after leaving the fight scene he remembered his wooden eye protector. All he could do was squint against the glare, and by the end of the afternoon he was snow-blind. By feel he cut a piece of skin from one of the packs and wrapped it around his head and over his eyes.

On and on they went, the half-conscious man clinging to the back of the sled, wracked with pain. Once, the dogs stopped and he realized they were resting. Somehow he found the chunks of meat he had put on the sled and feeling his way along the harness, fed them. The last big chunk he gave to the muzzle that pushed itself into his hand. Lying on the sled, he slept until Shadow's nose nudged his mitten. Too weak to ride the runners, he lay there and called commands to the dogs. Miraculously, they rose and pulled against the harness…the sled was underway again. Some time later, a faint sound roused him.

"I spotted them a long way off. The wolf was in front, leading the sled dogs. He brought them home! And there's a seal under him!" Tikaani's voice brought Tukor out of his stupor. He felt hands lift him from the sled and gasped at the pain.

"Look at those slashes in his parka; only a bear could have done that." It was Qimmiq. "It's a miracle he survived; get him inside, he's badly hurt and seems to be snow-blind."

"Wait," Tukor croaked, his voice hardly recognizable, "backtrack the trail, there are two more seals and a bear to feed the children."

CHAPTER 21

Snowblind

JUAN AND SOPHIA SAT motionless, spellbound by the scene Great Grandfather had just described.

"How big do you think the bear was?" asked Juan.

"When I asked him the same question, my great grandfather said he thought it was at least 1,000 pounds."

"An animal that big must have been incredibly strong," observed the youth. "Why didn't the blow utterly crush Tukor's chest?"

"It would have, under normal circumstances" acknowledged the old man, "but for the armor shirt."

"He was wearing it?" asked a startled Juan.

"Yes. He told me the shirt was always his first layer during the winter because of the extreme cold."

"It's made of wool, so that makes sense," said Sophia. "But I've never thought of it before."

"That's because you have excellent one-piece snowmobile suits, long underwear, hand warmers and a thermos for hot chocolate," replied Great Grandfather. "And also because it doesn't get to minus 50 or minus 60 degrees around here anymore...and you're probably not going to run into a polar bear," he added with a grin.

"True," she agreed.

"Remember, Tukor wasn't used to the cold and always wore everything he had. When I was a kid, he'd tell me the weave of the armor shirt retained a lot of body heat, almost as much as the feather shirts," said their relative. "Anyway, when they got his clothes off him, his entire chest was black, blue, and yellow. Tikaani, Qimmiq, and the others were astounded he'd survived, much less made it home."

"But he wouldn't have made it home except for Shadow," said Juan. "You said he was collapsed on the sled when they came into view, and Tikaani spotted Shadow leading the sled dogs in. How did that happen?"

"I don't know,' replied Great Grandfather. "Except the wolf was the alpha male and somehow those huskies followed him."

"How long did it take Tukor to recover?" Sophia wanted to know.

"By the time Yutu's people joined the other bands for the summer camp, he was able to hunt, but his eyes never fully recovered. He had to wear some kind of protection against bright light for the rest of his life. Because of it, his hunting was restricted to dawn and dusk, but he was as deadly as ever with the sling."

"What about Shadow?" she asked.

"He seemed to sense Tukor's vision problems and stayed closer than ever before. They spent the next summer with the reunited village; then Qimmiq and Tikaani guided them back to the Makah when the rivers froze. By the end of the following summer, Tukor and the wolf were back in the canyons," explained Great Grandfather. "Shadow lived for many years and died peacefully one night lying beside the man he loved. Unfortunately, it happened years before I was born but the carved wolf in my great grandfather's house made Shadow almost as real in my imagination as if I'd known him personally."

CHAPTER 22

New Home

SPRING HAD TURNED TO summer and the twins spent as much time as possible fly fishing, but they never missed a Saturday morning session with Great Grandfather. When he finished the story of Tukor, the twins plied him with questions about his own life after he and his father made friends with the Rodriguez family. Although he had told them they should know about the life of the Wearer immediately prior to them, he seemed reluctant to talk about himself. Reminded by them of this earlier statement, he finally agreed they should have a complete understanding of the family history.

Leaning back in the rocking chair, after biscuits and honey butter one morning, his eyes took on that familiar distant look as he focused on the past....

The same winter Ricardo received the medallion, he and his father rode back to the Rodriguez' hacienda. Carlos had been so impressed with the teaching Bruno received from his grandmother that he asked if she'd be willing to include his son. The promise of ten fine horses, to be delivered over the next two years, sealed the arrangement and Ricardo settled in at the hacienda.

From then on, the two boys spent three hours every morning with Christa. At the end of 24 months, the results were extraordinary: both could read and write at an advanced level, were starting geometry, and had an amazing grasp of North American and world history learned through books delivered from Mexico City and Santa Fe. In a day when many ranch children had limited access to schools, Christa's knowledge and skills had the two boys approaching a high school education while they were still nine years old.

When Armando became ill, Ricardo returned home to help his father with the horses. After the culture and education of the Rodriguez' household, the simple life in the canyons was a bit strange, but he quickly lost himself in the work of training horses. Carlos' foresight about education proved providential, however, when disaster struck the spring Ricardo turned ten. The first indication that something was wrong occurred when irrigation ditches to the gardens had to be deepened.

"We can't get enough water to the vegetables," explained the old woman who supervised the gardening. By the end of June, water in the creek was noticeably lower and the ditches had to be deepened again. At the end of August, there was barely a trickle flowing through the canyon. Out in the main canyon, the same thing was happening: the big creek was drying up.

"Cuto and Ria settled here almost 300 years ago," said Carlos one evening, sitting on a stump and watching great shadows creep out from the escarpment. "The water's never dried up."

"Perhaps that's why the Ancients abandoned the cliff dwelling," replied his lifelong friend Mendoza, who occupied one of the three white houses with his family. "We know they had gardens on the ground below, so there must have been water at that time. Maybe this is part of a cycle that has happened before."

"We'll have to leave also, unless it changes," said Carlos. "Without water for pastures, our horses won't survive."

"What will you do?"

"Ricardo and I are leaving tomorrow for the Rodriguez' hacienda. I think they will temporarily pasture the herd if we supply extra men. I've an idea where we can go, but I need time to explore it."

"The vaqueros and I will go wherever you need, Patrón," said Mendoza. "Generations of us owe a great debt to your family." A few days later, when Carlos explained his predicament to Jorge Rodriguez, the latter offered his complete support.

"If you need, I'll send men to help move the herd," he said. "We can keep the animals for as long as you like."

"Thank you, my friend. I've enough men to bring the herd and tend it, but after we get the horses settled, I'm taking the train to southern Colorado. There's a valley my ancestors knew about where we might be able to relocate."

A month later, when Carlos stepped off the train in a little town called Alamosa, a towering mountain range to the east immediately caught his attention. It rose abruptly from the floor of the massive valley, jagged peaks thrusting at the sky with traces of snow still showing despite the August heat. It was exactly as Lita, Rutu, Beast Blinder, and Tukor had described it. In an odd way, it felt almost like coming home. He unloaded his horse from the livestock car and spent the next two weeks exploring.

The buffalo were gone, and a few small farms had sprung up, but as he rode north he imagined Lita and Rutu herding wild horses toward Badger Snarling and the hidden villagers waiting to haze them into the trap. At the far end of the valley a wagon road climbed toward a distant pass; he wondered whether it followed the trail his ancestors had ridden to seek the ocean.

To the west of Alamosa flowed the Rio Grande and as he followed it a few days later, Carlos chuckled over the story of Rutu stepping into the deceptively deep, clear water. Near its headwaters he came to the town of Creede: once a silver boomtown, but now a mining center for the less glamorous lead and zinc.

On Pinos Creek, west of the tiny settlement of Del Norte, he found what he was looking for: a long, narrow valley with lush bottomland. Down it flowed a beautiful stream reminiscent of home. It was perfect for the horses. Six weeks later the herd was trailed north and settled into the abundant meadows bordering Pinos Creek. A number of families from the canyon came north with Carlos and work began on a headquarters for the ranch.

CHAPTER 23
Rock Dog

RICARDO SPOTTED THE rider on the crest of the ridge west of their cabin. He was helping his father and the men expand what had been a small hunting cabin into a three-bedroom home. Armando, now fully recovered, had excellent carpentry skills and Mendoza had a knack for chinking; under their supervision a team was making rapid progress on the building. Other men were busy constructing corrals and clearing an area for a barn. When Ricardo glanced again at the ridge, the rider was gone. The next day he was back, but in a different spot. Thereafter, hardly a day went by without the horseman appearing on the western skyline. Finally Ricardo decided to clear up the mystery.

"Ease up there on a horse," advised his father. "It's obviously someone who's curious about what we're doing here."

The next day, the boy secured a horse from the herd and, when the rider appeared, mounted it and slowly approached the ridge. As he drew closer, he was surprised to see that the rider was an Indian boy about his own age. Both of them were bareback and Ricardo observed the Indian was completely at home on his animal. In fact, the two boys could have been related: Ricardo still favored the knee-high moccasins, loose clothing, and headband of people from the pueblos; the other, dressed in buckskins and moccasins, also sported a headband. The two stared at each other for several minutes.

"Why are you watching us?" asked Ricardo in Spanish. The boy shook his head and said something Ricardo couldn't understand. The New Mexican repeated his question in English.

"I report to my people what the men with beautiful horses are doing," replied the youth. "We hope you are going to stay. We would like to acquire some of your animals."

"My family has trained horses for generations in the desert," said Ricardo, glad to have the language barrier removed. "But our water dried up and we had to move the herd. This will be our new home."

"Good. Water won't be a problem; we get a lot of snow each winter."

"I know," Ricardo answered. When the other looked surprised, he went on. "Some of my ancestors spent time in this area and brought back stories of snow. What's your name?"

"Rock Dog," replied the other solemnly.

"My name is Ricardo. Do you live nearby?"

"My people live on the Rio Grande, a little to the west," replied the boy, turning his horse away. "I have to go now."

"Tomorrow, you must come down to the cabin. I'll show you what we're doing," said Ricardo.

"I will," said Rock Dog. Thus began a friendship destined to last for decades.

At first, Rock Dog visited the growing headquarters of Carlos' ranch. In time, however, Ricardo was invited to the little cluster of teepees and small houses about five miles away. A number of elders in the village continued to live in teepees, but Rock Dog's family lived in one of the houses. Ricardo was enchanted with the Indian's four-year-old sister, Butterfly, who reminded him of little Gissy back at the hacienda.

The Indians kept asking Ricardo about horses and one day, three months later, Carlos and his son brought four animals to the village. The entire community turned out to study the horses, commenting on their sleek and powerful appearance.

"We prize good horses," said Rock Dog's father, Horse Rearing. "These animals are better than any we can find in the Valley."

"A long time ago we began breeding and training horses for specific uses," replied Carlos. "I think you'll be impressed with their performance."

"First a barbeque," the Indian smiled. "We want our guests well fed!"

The village numbered about 50 men, women, and children. Soon great mounds of food filled tables set up under the cottonwoods at the river's edge and everyone gathered for the feast. During the meal, the conversation centered on horses and it was clear the Indians hoped to do business with the newcomers.

CHAPTER 24

Connections

When the food was cleared, the entire population moved to a flat, grassy area some distance away. The elders, most in traditional dress, sat on blankets; the younger men, some in jeans, boots, and hats, squatted nearby watching the riders intently.

Carlos and Ricardo put each of the horses through a variety of exercises on a simple course they had created with rocks. A few of the demonstrations, such as sideways agility and head-on charges, dated back to the days of war and buffalo hunting. Others were more tailored to modern use: abrupt stops followed by rapid backing, pivoting from side to side on hind legs, slow figure eights. As was their custom, the New Mexicans rode bareback but for a small pad. The horses wore a hackamore with a continuous-rein loop connected to it. The riders often dropped the rein and conducted drills hands-free to demonstrate their mounts' responses to knee pressure and body position.

The final exercise was a throwback to the days when a warrior might want to rescue a fallen comrade. A sack of potatoes on the ground was approached at a dead run. The rider, one hand gripping the horse's mane and one foot tucked across its back, leaned close to the ground and snatched up the sack as he raced past. It was an impressive demonstration and the watching crowd erupted in applause. When Ricardo performed the feat with his second horse, the medallion slipped out from under his shirt as he leaned over to grab the sack.

As he trotted his horse back to the audience, Ricardo realized that every eye was on him and the previously enthusiastic Indians were totally silent and motionless. Slipping off the horse, he dropped the sack and looked at his father in confusion. But Carlos was as bewildered as his son.

"What is it you wear under your shirt?" asked an elder sitting in front of them. He was very old, with a deeply wrinkled face and white hair. Ricardo looked at his father; the medallion often popped out during horse training and he'd replaced it with no thought.

"Show them, Son," murmured Carlos, an impossible idea beginning to form. When his son pulled out the medallion, there was an audible gasp from the assembled village. A rapid exchange ensued among the elders in a language neither of their visitors could understand. Finally the old man spoke.

"The legends are true," he began. "They've been passed down for generations: tales of people from the south who wore an odd piece of silver. They saved our ancestors from starvation after the great disease and provided us with our first horses. They used strange weapons and one of them married into the tribe and came to live with us. He became one of our greatest leaders."

"The stories are not legend," replied Carlos. "Our family has worn this medallion for almost 400 years and passed down its history to each generation, just as your village has done. An ancestor and her brother came to the valley and met Badger Snarling, whose people were nearly dead." At the mention of the Ute name, there was another gasp from the people and excited whispers were exchanged as the people grasped the import of Carlos' words.

"Lita and Rutu killed buffalo for them and eventually trapped their first wild horses. Our family reports that Badger Snarling always kept an empty lodge for their return." The old man nodded.

"My grandfather said that the practice was maintained faithfully and, when he was a young child, another came wearing the medallion. The stories say he was accompanied by a great black wolf."

"That was Tukor," acknowledged Carlos. "He and his wolf traveled all the way to the Arctic."

"Ahh," replied the elder with satisfaction. "We tell that he fought an enormous white bear, but there is no such animal around here so we believed the ancestors were mistaken."

"The polar bear would have killed him but for the wolf," explained Carlos. "Tukor was my grandfather; he died peacefully a year ago." The Ute looked at him in astonishment.

"But I am much older than you and my grandfather was a child when Tukor came through. He must have lived to a very old age!"

"Those who wear the medallion outlive the rest of us by many years," Carlos explained.

CHAPTER 25

War

A YEAR AFTER THE RANCH was firmly established on Pinos Creek, his father sent Ricardo back to the Rodriguez hacienda to continue his education. They had tried the one-room school in Del Norte, but quickly discovered that Christa's instruction had advanced the boy's knowledge far beyond what the local teacher could offer. Once again, he and Bruno spent most mornings on the patio studying math, history, and literature; Christa teaching in both Spanish and English to prepare her students for what they might encounter later on. Afternoons were spent helping with the large herds of cattle Jorge Rodriguez had acquired, or hunting if the occasion arose. When he took the train home at Christmas, Armando and the others questioned Ricardo about the canyons.

"Bruno and I rode there," he explained, "but we had to take a pack horse with two barrels of water. The creeks are totally dry and the pastures have turned to dust; even the houses are starting to crumble. It looks like no one has lived there for 100 years. The villagers who didn't move here have all gone to Santa Fe."

"There's no need to worry about water in Pinos Creek," said Mendoza, as they hauled hay to the herd on sleds through three feet of snow. "But the cold takes getting used to."

Eighteen months later, Christa sent Ricardo north with a letter saying she could teach him nothing more; university would be the next step. Carlos was pleased. He knew there was a university in Denver which could prepare his son for all the changes taking place in the world. By now, 1910, automobiles were common in Alamosa and newspapers were reporting the progress of airplanes. New inventions were being promoted for planting crops and putting up hay. Carlos knew Ricardo would become their guide into the modern world.

Home again, his son re-established his friendship with Rock Dog and the two were nearly inseparable. Ever since the New Mexican's first horse demonstration, the Ute boy had been determined ride like his friend. Although he was a good rider, Rock Dog hadn't been raised on horseback like Ricardo and he turned to Armando for help while the other boy was gone. By the time Ricardo returned to the ranch, the Ute had become nearly his equal with horses. They began traveling with the vaqueros to local roping competitions and before long the two 15 year-olds were among the top hands in the area.

In the fall of 1910, Ricardo traveled to Denver on the train and enrolled at the University of Denver. He was three years younger than most first-year students, but equal to, or ahead of them in almost every course. Over the next three years, his fluency in Spanish and Indian dialects caught the attention of Mr. Cisneros, a professor of archaeology. The professor took Ricardo under his wing. He invited him for dinner with his wife and family and they got to know about each other's lives. As Mr. Cisneros learned about Ricardo's Inca and Aztec background, the boy in turn became fascinated with the professor's descriptions of other ancient peoples around the globe. When Ricardo graduated, just three years later, the professor encouraged him to return for an advanced degree in archaeology.

Summers were spent working on the ranch with Rock Dog, now one of Carlos' valued trainers. There was no lack of buyers for the well-schooled horses and the two friends were often charged with delivering the animals by rail to places as far away as California, Wyoming, and Texas. By 1913, the newspapers were full of stories of international tensions in Europe and in the summer of 1914, a year after Ricardo graduated, war broke out. It had an immediate impact on the horse business.

Buyers for the English and French armies showed up in Del Norte; they needed good horses for the war in Europe and Carlos' herd bordered on legendary. In the beginning, the rancher resisted their offers. In September, however, a representative for the British Army arrived and refused to take no for an answer, renting rooms in a local hotel. After three weeks of daily visits, his offer for the entire herd of 300 horses had risen to an astronomical amount. Carlos gathered his most trusted advisors at the ranch house one night.

"Patrón, keep two stallions and five mares," counseled Armando. "We can build another herd."

"The man is crazy," said Mendoza. "No herd is worth that much money. He'll change his mind in the morning."

"No," said Ricardo. "The man is not crazy. It is a matter of supply and demand. The English desperately need horses for this Great War and they have limited options. If this man doesn't get our horses, the French will." He looked at the others. "At the University, I studied the politics that led to this war. Setting aside the business aspect, the English are our allies and we should do what we can to help them."

Carlos looked at his son with admiration.

"Our family has always helped its friends. I will accept the offer tomorrow."

Within a week Ricardo and Rock Dog departed for England with a trainload of horses. Only a handful of mounts, and 10 animals of breeding stock, remained on Pinos Creek.

CHAPTER 26
England

WHEN THE HERD WAS finally delivered to the English Army base, Ricardo discovered that word had gone ahead and the horses were slated for officers only. Carlos had been told that his men might have to train ordinary soldiers to ride the animals, but the officer corps was a different matter: every man was an accomplished rider and appreciated the fine horses from America. The result was that Ricardo and Rock Dog (adjusted to "Mr. Rock Dog" for the British) were free for several weeks before they could catch a ship back to the United States. Near the horse facilities where they were housed was an aerodrome. Planes fascinated Ricardo and the two young men spent hours in front of the hangers watching men learning to fly. In their cowboy hats, jeans, and boots, and with their quiet, polite demeanors, the pair soon became favorites with the pilots. Wild west shows had toured Europe and the Brits were as curious about the Americans as the Americans were about them. One day in October, Reginald Butterworth, Commander of the reconnaissance group training at the aerodrome, approached the Americans.

"I say, chaps, don't be surprised if you hear the sound of firing from behind the hangars," he began. "We're testing a new machine gun to be carried on the planes. Has to fire backwards, though, because they haven't discovered how to shoot forward through the propeller spin. Bit of a problem, don't you know, if you shot yourself down by shredding the propeller." He smiled at them through the pipe clenched in his teeth.

"We hadn't realized you were going to arm the planes," said Ricardo. "We thought they were just for spotting troop movements on the ground."

"That's how it began, but the Germans have been harassing our planes with their own aircraft. The men have been carrying revolvers and rifles, but the revolvers aren't accurate enough and the rifles difficult to handle while controlling the plane."

"I'd imagine," responded Rock Dog, putting a hand to his mouth to hide a smile. It was hard enough to shoot a rifle off a horse; he couldn't imagine what it would be like while trying to control an airplane.

"Word is the Germans are also working on a machine gun for their planes; if they succeed before we do, they'll be able to shoot our men out of the sky. Nasty business that would be," muttered the officer. "Oh, and take care to announce yourselves to the sentries," he said.

"Sentries?" said Ricardo in surprise. "We've not run into any sentries."

"The machine guns are very hush, hush, you know, so we're posting sentries to guard against spies."

"Spies?" echoed the Ute.

"Yes, we executed one the other day at the Tower of London."

"I read about that," replied Ricardo. "It seems the enemy is trying to learn your secrets."

"And we theirs," acknowledged the Englishman with a smile. "The two of you are well known to all of us, but the sentries are new, so be sure to announce yourselves, particularly in the dark." Butterworth waved as he strolled back to the command shack.

There was a club at the flying field where the airmen gathered at night, and the two horsemen were fond of joining their new friends to learn about the war's progress, share stories of the American West, and teach them cowboy songs. That night, as they announced their presence to the new sentry on the airfield perimeter, Ricardo was startled to feel warmth on his chest. He realized it was coming from the medallion.

Although he had been wearing it since he was seven, the silver piece had never once changed temperature. As they walked toward the club, the warmth gradually diminished and he wondered idly whether the artifact was helping warm him against the damp English cold. By the time they stepped inside, there was no sensation at all and he forgot about it. But it recurred later that night as they made their way home.

The next day a problem arose with the horses, causing the cowboys to spend a couple of days riding with the officers. The latter were complaining that their mounts didn't respond well to being reined.

"These horses have been trained differently than the ones you are used to," explained Ricardo to an assembly of riders in their starched uniforms. "A century ago, my family was training animals primarily for Indians, who were constantly at war with one another. In battle, a warrior needed both hands free to use a bow, lance, or possibly two tomahawks. Our horses have always been trained to respond to body movement as the primary source of guidance." He glanced at the field behind them where a long row of posts had been sunk in the ground.

"I see you're working on a saber course. Let me demonstrate." He turned to a nearby officer. "May I borrow your sword and your horse?" Armed with the man's weapon, Ricardo led the animal to the front of the group and removed its bridle. In one smooth motion he vaulted onto the small leather saddle and, not bothering with the stirrups, raced away toward the poles.

Normally the officers cantered along the same side of the poles going down the field and coming back; this allowed them to practice using the saber to the right of the horse on the way down and to the left on the way back. Ricardo's mount ran at full speed, with no visible guidance from the rider, weaving through the line of poles so Ricardo could alternate slashing them from either side. The horse spun on its back legs at the end of the line and wove its way back, coming to a sliding halt in front of the Englishmen. For a moment there was dead silence.

"I say, old fellow," said Colonel Figby, the ranking officer, "your family has the knack of it! I don't know that we'll take off the bridles, but we can dispense with a lot of reining."

"If you'll excuse me, may I make a suggestion?" asked the cowboy.

"Of course," replied Figby. Privately, the man had made fun of the Americans but he now realized these lean young men, dressed in their rough clothing, were superior to any riders in his command. Furthermore, they were impeccably polite: a trait that sat well with the English.

"With all due respect, sir," said Ricardo. "You might consider converting those two long reins into a single loop extending from one side of the bridle around the horse's neck to the other side. That way the soldier could drop the rein on the animal's neck and use one hand for a sword and the other for a pistol without dropping reins to the ground."

"What a capital idea!" cried the Colonel. "Both hands for fighting the Huns! We'll try it."

CHAPTER 27

Attack

As they prepared to go to the pilot's club that night, Ricardo glanced at the medallion when he changed shirts. He remembered its warmth three nights before and hesitated.

"The medallion will always warn you of danger," Tukor had said 12 years earlier when he passed on the piece of silver. Was it possible there was danger at the airfield? Butterworth had said they were experimenting with the new machine gun. He'd also said there were enemy spies in England. Ricardo rummaged in his duffle.

"What're you doing?" asked Rock Dog.

"I've a funny feeling about the airfield," explained his friend. He had told the Ute about his experience, but neither had given it much thought because of the mild nature of the sensation. "My great grandfather told me heat from the medallion was a sign of danger. I'm going to wear this under my clothing." He pulled out his armor shirt.

"What's that?" His friend had never seen the garment before.

"It's a type of armor," replied Ricardo. "It's a special weave from the Inca Empire that's been known to our family for centuries. It was used by warriors in battle against the conquistadors."

"Does it work?" The Ute asked doubtfully, fingered the material. "It feels like heavy wool."

"I don't know, I've never had to use it."

"Wear it," advised Rock Dog firmly. "Our legends include strange and wonderful tales of your family. If the medallion is warning you, you may need the shirt; if not, it will help against the damp cold."

When they approached the airfield boundary a cheerful voice, in what they now knew to be a Cockney accent, rang out.

"Hold up, lads. Where are you going?" A beam of light thrust through the dark onto their faces. "Oh, the cowboys, wot! Commander told me you might be coming through. Are you still at war with the Indians?"

"No," laughed Ricardo, "although my friend here has threatened to lift my scalp several times!"

"Keep that big hat on," advised the soldier. "He'll never be able to reach your hair. Have a care on your way to the club; it's rather dodgy getting around in the dark."

"Is the medallion warm?" murmured the Ute as they made their way across the grass runway toward the club.

"Not at all," replied Ricardo. Both completely forgot the matter as they were warmly greeted inside the building.

"We need to educate the English about a good steak," commented Rock Dog dryly as they left the club several hours later. "Their mutton and pot pie leave something to be desired."

"Maybe we could buy a steer from a local farmer and show them how it's done. What was that?" Ricardo stopped. A faint noise had come from the darkened hangar to their right.

"It sounded like someone dropped something," muttered the Ute.

"We better alert the sentry," said Ricardo as they headed toward the perimeter and spoke to the guard.

"Don't worry, sir. We'll take care of it," said the darkened figure as they approached. Although they were crossing the boundary at the same place, the cheerful Cockney accent was gone: the man in front of them had a deeper, rough voice. Suddenly, the medallion was hot. Ricardo grabbed Rock Dog's arm.

"I forgot my wallet at the club," he said. "Let's go back." As they started back across the runway, two figures loomed up behind them. Something was jammed so hard into Ricardo's back that he fell violently face forward with a cough. At the same time, Rock Dog gave a cry and crumpled to the ground. Before he could move, Ricardo heard a whispered voice.

"What'd you have to kill him for? We could have just tied them up and been done with it." It was the voice of the new sentry. There was a low, nasty laugh in reply.

"I just got this knife and I've always wanted to run someone through. Did you hear the coughing as he died?"

"These two are Americans," the whisper from the sentry was harsh. "They're not in the fight."

"Yeah, but they're helping the Brits."

"Let's drag the bodies over by the hangar and lend a hand to the others with the machine gun. Then I suppose we'll have to kill the the other one, but we'll let Helmut decide." Ricardo felt a hand grab his coat collar and he was dragged across the airfield to the looming shape of the hangar, where he was dropped beside a wall.

"You go inside and find the others," whispered the sentry, "I'll tie up the one I knocked out and join you."

"Why don't we just kill him right now?"

"Helmut's in charge. He'll make the decision. Now go!" There was a muttered curse as the killer left, then the sound of tape being unrolled and cut as Rock Dog was securely trussed up. Receding footsteps indicated the phony sentry's departure.

Ricardo rolled over and sat up. He felt along his back with one hand. There was a slit through his coat and heavy wool shirt, but it stopped there…the armor shirt had protected him. Apparently, the knife going through his heavy outer clothing, coupled with his forward fall and cough, had convinced his inexperienced assailant that the blade had pierced his body. There was no time to lose, however, because the spies might come back at any moment. Grabbing the unconscious Ute, he dragged him across the grass into the shadows of the neighboring hangar and cut him free with his pocket knife.

"Wait here," he whispered as the Indian began to groan. "Don't make a sound; I'll be back." An answering grip on his arm indicated Rock Dog understood and Ricardo moved swiftly toward the first hangar, loosening his coat and shirt as he went.

There were no lights around the airfield and clouds blocked most of the illumination from the half moon; nevertheless, the grass landing strip provided a slightly paler background than the dark bulk of the hangar. The American made preparations and crouched on the grass about 10 yards from the side door into the building. Minutes went by before he heard the tiny squeak of a hinge as the door was eased open.

For a moment, the black mass of the hanger hid everything; then the silhouettes of four men emerged against the backdrop of the runway. They were carrying something heavy between them. They paused in mid-stride as a strange whirring noise arose from the dark; suddenly one of the men in front dropped the object and fell to the ground, grasping his thigh with both hands and groaning loudly. Before the others had time to react, the strange noise started again and another man arched his back, throwing both hands in the air, and collapsed.

"Go." The voice was audible, as the last two men adjusted their grip and began hurrying away with their load. Again came the whirring and one of them screamed aloud and lost his grip on the object. He staggered a few steps and sank to the ground. The last man, unable to carry the load by himself, dropped it and tried to sprint away. He gained a few yards before falling to the grass with a shriek and writhing on his back. The noise alerted the sentries and flashlights dotted the field as they rushed toward the hanger.

"Over here!" called Ricardo, directing them toward the fallen thieves. The British sentries ran up with rifles leveled. "No need to shoot," said the American calmly. "They're not going anywhere." He stood in a pool of light, two strands of leather hanging from his right hand.

"Blimey, it's the cowboy!" came a familiar Cockney voice. "But he's lost his hat! Where's your friend?"

"He was knocked silly by these men," said Ricardo. "He's over by that hanger." In short order, two English soldiers were guiding Rock Dog into the light.

"What happened?" he grunted, sitting down and holding his head. By now flood-lights were blazing and pilots, having scrambled from their beds, were pouring from the barracks in various stages of undress.

"It seems we've had a wee incident," said Lieutenant Farnsworth, a Scot.

"Aye, but no damage done, thanks to the Americans," replied Lieutenant Peacock. "By Jove, they've lost their big white hats!" He spoke to the sentries. "Men, step lively now and retrieve those hats. These two look positively naked without them!"

CHAPTER 28

Assassins

"ONE BROKEN FEMUR, two cracked vertebrae, and a ruptured spleen," announced Butterworth the next morning. "I say chaps, that's quite an accomplishment. But the sentries report no discharge of a firearm."

"We left our firearms in Colorado," replied Ricardo as he and Rock Dog sat with the commander at breakfast, the Indian sporting white bandages around his head.

"The men said something about some sort of sling," Butterworth raised an eyebrow.

"Yes, sir" answered the American. "I've been using one since I was three."

"Extraordinary," mused the Brit. "I thought such ancient weapons had been abandoned long ago."

"Perhaps, in many places," said Ricardo. "But it has its advantages. It's relatively quiet and highly effective at 30–40 yards. I could have killed all four of those men, but I thought you'd like to question them."

"Quite so," said the Commander. "Our men are doing exactly that right now. But how did you come to use such a weapon?"

"My family was originally Inca," explained Ricardo. "The sling was the weapon preferred over lances and bows. It can drop a horse, kill a man, or be used to throw firebombs. For the past 400 years, every member in our family line has been trained with it." Reginald stared at him.

"I thought the English had long family histories. Four HUNDRED years, you say?"

"That's not all," interjected Rock Dog. "His family and my people have been associated for nearly 300 years." He grinned. "Europeans are not the only ones to trace back their lineages!"

"Do you use the sling also?" inquired Butterworth.

"No, until the advent of firearms, we used the bow and the lance. Both are formidable from horseback."

"Ahh, the English have a long history with the bow and the lance, though neither are practiced much anymore. Perhaps the two of you should visit our museum to see the weapons we've used through the centuries."

"We'd like that very much," replied Ricardo.

Two days later the cowboys toured The British Museum, accompanied by a British corporal in starched uniform. Their big hats, wool shirts, jeans, and boots, attracted many a discrete stare, but the young men were oblivious as they took in historical exhibits from around the world. Ricardo, in particular, was captivated by artifacts he'd only imagined while at the University of Denver and resolved to pursue the study of archaeology when he got home. That night the two talked animatedly about what they'd seen, including taxidermied animals, Egyptian mummies, Roman chariots, and Persian carvings.

During their last two weeks in England the cowboys once more encountered peril. After another trip to The British Museum, they were strolling back toward their quarters when the medallion suddenly turned hot.

"Stop," muttered Ricardo to Rock Dog and the lance corporal accompanying them. "Something's wrong." It was completely dark, due to the blackout in London, but just ahead of them was an alley containing shops which he and Rock Dog often visited during the day. The three stepped back against the building on their left, the alley only a few yards ahead.

"No need for your weapon," whispered the American to the soldier, who was fumbling for his revolver. "Stay here with Mr. Rock Dog. I'm crossing the street."

In spite of the advice, the Brit freed his pistol and stood quietly beside the Ute. Like a shadow, their companion moved across the dark street. Ricardo was able to take advantage of a doorway opposite the alley to peer into it, but the shadows were too dense to see anything. But heat from the medallion alerted him that danger lurked in the gloom. Suddenly, a momentary rent in the clouds allowed a bit of starlight to shine and he saw them: six men crouched against the walls. Three were on one side of the narrow passage and three on the other.

When the strange whirring began, the six assassins stiffened and gripped their clubs, but there was nothing visible to attack, even though one of them slumped to the pavement coughing and retching.

"Good Lord," whispered another. "What was that?" He shrunk against the wall as the noise began again. There was a clatter as another man dropped his club and pitched face forward to the ground.

"We can't just stand here," growled the leader and advanced out of the alley as the whirring started again. His scream shredded the silence as a shattered knee gave way under him.

"Run!" shouted one of the remaining assailants. "They didn't pay us enough for this!" Pounding footsteps sounded on the cobblestones as the last three fled up the alley.

"It's over," Ricardo called to his companions, the medallion cool again on his skin. "I suppose we'd better find one of your Bobbies."

"Crikey! I'd heard about that sling of his, but never believed it could be so effective," exclaimed the soldier to Rock Dog.

"Those men don't know it," replied the Ute, "but they're lucky to be alive."

It took a while to find a policeman in the darkened streets, but before long the three were on their way home. The soldier was still incredulous over what the cowboy had done.

"How can you be so accurate in the dark?" he asked.

"It's like everything else: practice," said the American. "Almost every day since I was a 'wee one,' as you would say. With that much practice you could do the same."

"But it was almost pitch black! How could you make out the targets?"

"There was a brief instant of starlight when I spotted them against the walls. After that, I could make out the bulk of their bodies so I just threw at the mass of the first two. At close range, the rock will do damage wherever it hits; I suspect the first man has broken ribs and the second some kind of internal injury," Ricardo speculated. "The third was easy because when he stepped into the street I could see his profile clearly enough to take aim."

"Blimey," said the Englishman in awe, "the Bobbies said they'd need an ambulance to take those three to the hospital. Your Indian friend says they're lucky to be alive."

"I don't think it's wise to be killing citizens of another country," chuckled the cowboy. "It's not good for international relations."

CHAPTER 29

Honored by the Crown

"THOSE BLOKES WERE common thugs from the docks," explained Reginald Butterworth two days later. "They told the police they'd been offered a big payment for killing the two cowboys with white hats staying at the horse compound. They weren't given any reason, although that kind doesn't need a reason; I suspect it had to do with your disruption of the machine gun theft."

"We were lucky, I guess," said Ricardo noncommittally. He'd made no mention of the medallion to anyone in England.

"Well, it was a nasty business, but you and that archaic weapon of yours saved the day once again."

"Modern firearms outperform it," acknowledged the cowboy. "But it has its advantages," he grinned. Turning serious, he extended a hand toward the commander. "We're heading back to America the day after tomorrow, but we both want to express our appreciation for the courtesies you all have shown us during our visit."

"My dear fellows, the pleasure has been entirely ours," replied the Commander. "In fact, we've planned a small going-away party for you tomorrow at 3:00 PM. We hope very much you'll attend." He raised an eyebrow.

"We'd be delighted," said Ricardo, borrowing a phrase they'd often heard from the Brits during their time in England. The Americans gave the slightest bow of their heads and touched the brims of their hats with their right hands. As they strolled toward their quarters, each made sure to maintain an impassive face. They'd been practicing the move in secret for 10 days, but this was their first opportunity to use British formality with an officer. Delighted as they were with themselves, neither suspected Butterworth's reaction.

"I'd take either of them under my command at any time," Reginald thought as he watched them walk away.

Tipped off by Lieutenant Farnsworth that the party would be "a wee bit formal," the Americans arrived at the airfield the next afternoon in freshly laundered white shirts, pressed jeans, and highly polished boots.

"'Small party,' indeed," muttered Ricardo. "Will you look at that!" In the middle of the grass runway a low platform had been erected. On one side of it stood Colonel Figby, clad in the formal military dress of a cavalry officer, sword at his side. A few paces to his right stood Commander Butterworth in the ceremonial uniform of the Air Corps, sword also at his side. At the edge of runway facing them stood a block of men in full military dress, 20 wide and three rows deep: the squadron pilots. On either side of the pilots was a row of horsemen, 20 wide and four rows deep: boots, saddles and brass polished to a high gloss, immaculate uniforms bright blue and red in the afternoon sun.

"That's quite a sight isn't it?" whispered a familiar Cockney voice as the airfield sentry appeared beside them. "Follow me, gents." He led them to the two low steps onto the platform. Holding his rifle straight before him with two hands, he addressed the officers in a clear voice.

"Your guests have arrived sirs: Mr. Ricardo and Mr. Rock Dog."

"Very well, show them up," replied Figby, neither man taking his eyes from the assembled troops. The soldier stepped to the side, rifle still in front of him, and nodded his head toward the platform.

"Up you go," he murmured, his voice barely audible. As the cowboys climbed the steps, both officers swung a quarter turn to face them, heels clicking audibly. After a tiny pause, both suddenly relaxed and stepped forward to shake hands with the Americans.

"We're so glad you could join us," said Butterworth. "We shall begin. Sergeant Major, please bring the men to order." From behind the stand emerged a heavyset soldier with a flaming red handlebar mustache. He marched to a position directly at the bottom of the platform steps.

"Eyes front!" he thundered in a voice that carried over the entire airfield. As one, the pilots, who had been standing in a somewhat leisurely posture, snapped to rigid attention. There was a strident ring as every horse-man removed his sword from its scabbard and snapped it into place against his right shoulder. The soldier pivoted to face the platform. "The men are in order sir."

"Thank you, Sergeant Major," replied the Commander as the man swung back to face the troops. In a voice almost as loud as the sergeant's, he addressed the assembly.

"We are here today to honor two men from the United States for exemplary service to England." He stepped back and Colonel Figby took over, with equal volume.

"Sent to deliver a vital cargo of horses for our officers, not only did they prove themselves equal as horsemen, but they taught us some techniques that will elevate us over the enemy in battle." At this, there was a loud "Huzzah" from the riders.

"Fortunately for us," he continued, "but unfortunately for them, they brought their entire herd, so there will be no mounts for them when they return to the frontier. However, men like these can ride anything the wild prairies of America offer up!" Three "Huzzahs" erupted from the mounted men. Butterworth took over.

"Not satisfied with flesh and blood, these men became fascinated with the idea of riding our winged machines," he began. "They befriended you pilots and spent many hours at the club learning about your skills." A loud cheer erupted from the pilots. "As you know, enemy spies attempted to steal our experimental machine gun and would have succeeded but for the efforts of the Americans. A later attempt on their lives was similarly thwarted." An even louder cheer from the airmen as the Commander paused. From behind the hangers a military band struck up a series of rousing marches.

"Normally, we would have had them in front of the stand but we weren't sure how your horses would react," muttered Figby.

"I'm not sure myself," murmured Ricardo, "we didn't play music for them."

"Not even songs of the warpath," added Rock Dog.

"Better safe than sorry." commented the Colonel, "We wouldn't want to ruin the occasion with a stampede." When the music stopped, he addressed the troops again.

"For service to England and for exemplary bravery, the Crown has approved the presentation to each of these men of a patch of the British flag, with the Royal Crest of England embroidered on it." The entire field erupted in cheer after cheer as the Sergeant Major mounted the platform and handed each officer a small box covered in black velvet. Butterworth stood in front of Ricardo and Figby before Rock Dog. Each removed a patch from the box, four inches long by three inches wide, and pinned it on the left shirt pocket of the cowboys. The officers shook hands with each American.

"Congratulations, gentlemen," said Figby. "The King recognizes our debt to you."

CHAPTER 30
The Patch

GREAT GRANDFATHER leaned back in the rocking chair and stared into space, lost in memories.

"The King?" stammered Juan. "The King of England knew about what you'd done?"

"It seems King George V had quite an interest in the American west," explained the old man with a smile. "Somehow, word reached him that two cowboys had delivered a shipment of horses to his officers and he actually considered inviting us to Buckingham Palace for tea. The pressures of war intervened and the invitation was never issued; however, the spy incident was brought to his attention and it was his idea to have the patches presented as an expression of the Crown's appreciation."

"You've got to be kidding," said Juan, "a gift from the King of England? Do you still have it?"

"Now, *you've* got to be kidding," Great Grandfather grinned. "Do you think I would lose something like that?" He rose and entered the house, returning shortly with a small black box. He handed it to Sophia.

"It's perfectly preserved," she said in awe, staring at the velvet covering.

"It's been wrapped in soft buckskin all these years," said her relative.

"May I open it?"

"Of course." Sophia opened the lid and stared, not daring to remove the patch. "It's beautiful," she murmured, handing the box to her brother. The cloth patch was the blue, red and white British Flag, over which had been embroidered in gold the Royal Crest of England. The Crest had a white unicorn standing on its hind legs holding up the right side of the Royal Shield, and a crowned lion standing on its hind legs holding up the left. The colors were as bright as they were on the day the patch was made.

"This is amazing!" exclaimed Juan, holding the box reverently in both hands. He stared at Great Grandfather. "You've never told us about any of these things."

"It wasn't time for my story before," said Great Grandfather. "You had to learn the history of your ancestors first."

"Yes, but we've never heard talk about your past from anyone!"

"These things happened a long, long time ago," said the old man. "The world's changed a lot since then."

""The world's changed a lot since Adzul got the medallion," countered Sophia. "Your history is as important as any of the Wearers." Juan handed the box back to Great Grandfather.

"What happened when you got home?"

"Come back next Saturday and I'll tell you," Great Grandfather's eyes wrinkled. "The two of you would have me spend the whole day on stories! I've got work to do!"

A week later, blueberry coffee cake and cantaloupe awaited the twins at the immaculate white house. Between bites, Juan described the monster Brown Trout his sister had landed with her fly rod Wednesday evening on the Rio Grande.

"She had to follow it downstream for at least 100 yards before I could net it," he explained. "At times she was almost waist deep in the river. For a while, I didn't dare leave her side because I thought she'd slip and go under. But the new sandals we've got have a great non-slip sole and she managed to stay upright until she could get it out of the current."

"Are you using sandals with your waders? I thought you had studded boots to go with them."

"No, in the summer we generally wear shorts and sandals; the air's warm and the water feels good. If you go under, at least you don't have to worry about the waders filling up and pulling you down."

"Well, you could always let go of the rod if you go under," replied their relative with an innocent expression. The two stared at him as if he'd lost his mind.

"And lose the fish?" cried Sophia. "We'll swim downstream with the rod before losing the fish!"

"I thought you might say something like that," chuckled Great Grandfather. "Just checking to make sure."

"Well, it measured a bit over 26 inches, three inches longer than anything I've caught this summer," said Juan, slightly mollified that the old man was just teasing. "Even after such a fight, when she released it there was a flick of the big tail and it was gone!"

"So, your sister's ahead in the competition this summer?" asked Great Grandfather. He knew that the two vied all summer for size and quantity of trout hooked and landed.

"I'm a little ahead in numbers, but she smoked me on size with that Brown," exclaimed Juan, obviously proud of his twin.

"There's a lot of fishing left," said Sophia, "and he usually gets a big one in the fall. But enough about fishing; what happened when you got back from England?"

As he had done so many times in the past two years, the old man sipped his coffee and his eyes took on a distant look.

"Rock Dog and I returned to Alamosa during a blizzard in the winter of 1915...," he began.

CHAPTER 31
Sling Skill

Carlos, Armando, and Horse Rearing were on the platform when the train pulled into Alamosa in a virtual whiteout. The men carried heavy Mackinaw overcoats and scarves for the young cowboys who descended from the railroad car with their valises and received bear hugs. Inside the depot, Ricardo and Rock Dog exchanged their long English coats for the much warmer garments the others had brought.

"We were wondering whether we'd freeze to death before we could get to the General Store for coats," exclaimed Ricardo, holding hands toward the hot potbelly stove in the station. "That train was bloody cold!" The older men noted a slight English accent to his words and smiled at one another. It was clear the time in Great Britain had impacted the young men.

"We came in last night because of weather conditions," said Carlos. "Even pulling a sled, the horses could barely make it. We've got rooms at the hotel for as long as the storm lasts and you're just in time for supper."

That night, over coffee in front of a crackling fire in the lobby's huge fireplace, the men sat spellbound over details of the cowboys' months away from home. There had been the long rail trip to New York City, followed by three weeks of maintaining the herd in a stockyard until the British located a ship. A number of men from the ranch had made the trip to New York, but returned to Colorado once the ship set sail. During the seven-day Atlantic crossing, Ricardo and Rock Dog were assisted by a few sailors with feeding and watering the horses. Fortunately, the weather stayed clear and travel was smooth. The ship landed at Plymouth and, once again, there were delays in finding train transport to the cavalry detachment at Newport. Upon arrival at Newport, they had learned that the horses were intended for officers and their training commitment would be minimal. This, of course, led to their introduction to the airfield and the subsequent events.

During the next two days, while the storm raged, the two young men recounted their experiences over and over to the fascinated men from home. Horse Rearing knew nothing about the use of a sling and insisted on examining the weapon in detail.

"It's nothing but two lengths of rawhide attached to a pouch!" he exclaimed in surprise. "How can this be such a deadly weapon?" No matter how much the others, including his son, tried to explain it to him he remained dubious. Finally, there was nothing that would convince him but a demonstration.

"How about using the stables?" suggested Carlos. "There's a long alleyway between the stalls and it's out of the storm." So the five of them trudged three blocks to the stables, barely able to see where they were going in the blinding snow. Once inside they were sheltered from the storm, but only a single lantern shed light in the otherwise dark and cavernous building. Sure enough, there was a long alley between the stalls and horses poked their heads over the doors as the men entered. In the little office, heated by yet another pot-belly stove, the stable manager offered them a cup of coffee, eager for the chance to visit.

"No one's been around for three days with this storm," he explained, as they gathered at the stove. "It gets lonely in here. So, you're the boys who went to England with the horses; your dad told me you were coming back when he dropped off the sled and team. I always wondered what it was like over there, them being our forefathers so to speak."

"For one thing, they love cowboys so they made us feel right at home," replied Ricardo.

"They love Indians too," added Rock Dog. "But their food isn't the best, except for the baked goods. They make these little pastries and breads for afternoon tea—delicious but tiny, and there's never enough! We never did see a steak!" When they'd finished their coffee, Carlos asked the manager if they could have a lantern to light the alleyway for a demonstration.

"Sure," answered the man, glad for any diversion from the monotony of the storm. He lit two lanterns and led the way to the stalls. The alley was nearly 50 feet long, with a big door at the end to access the corral outside. Carlos hung one lantern from a hook and walked to the far end to hang the other. By now, all the horses had their heads over the half doors like an audience. The dim flicker hardly illuminated the cavernous space, but did show the small can of Prince Albert tobacco Carlos placed on the stone floor.

""That's a pretty small target," remarked Horse Rearing as the rancher rejoined them.

"Yeah, but you can see it," said his son. "On the airfield and in the alley you could hardly see anything." The stableman watched curiously as Ricardo opened his Mackinaw and drew out the sling.

"What's that?" he wanted to know.

"It's an ancient weapon," answered Carlos. "Stand clear and watch." Loading the sling, Ricardo gave it four revolutions and fired. At the far end of the alley, the small can shot into the air and hit the door with a faint clang.

"I'm going to need another tobacco can," said Carlos dryly, observing that the tin was neatly bent in two.

"That's pretty good," acknowledged Horse Rearing. "But a warrior could hit that can with an arrow every time from this distance." Carlos stared at him, then turned to the stableman.

"Have you got an old horseshoe around here?"

"Yup," answered the man, walking to a nearby wall on which were hung a variety of tools. "How about this?" He held out a big thick horseshoe. "Got it off a plow horse."

"No, we need something smaller," was the answer. The man rummaged among some debris at the bottom of the wall and returned with a very small horseshoe.

"This came from a pony that the Mayor uses to pull a cart with his kids in it."

"Perfect," said Carlos. "Have you got an old length of rein we can use to hang it in the doorway down there?" A piece of leather was found and they hung the little horseshoe in the doorway at the end of the alley, about five feet above the floor. "Now open the doors."

"In this storm? The wind's fierce out there," argued the manager.

"Okay, just pull them back about four feet; they don't have to be wide open." With help from the boys, the manager slid the big doors back on their rollers until there was a four-foot opening. Immediately, the wind swirled inside and set the horseshoe swinging around. "That's good!" shouted the rancher against the roar of the storm and they regrouped at the head of the alley.

"Impossible," muttered Horse Rearing, as he watched the wildly swinging target. Ricardo searched the stable floor and found a stone larger than the ones he carried in his sack. He examined it closely against the light.

"This should do," he remarked, placing it in the sling. He studied the action of the horseshoe for a couple of minutes before setting the weapon in motion. The straps became a blur and the whir was audible above the noise of the storm. Round and round sped the sling until suddenly he released it.

There was a loud "clang" from the doorway and the target disappeared into the whiteness outside. It swung back into the opening on its leather cord as the men hurried down the alley to shut the doors and examine it. The metal was bent back almost a half inch, precisely at the middle of the curve where it was tied to the leather.

"Lucky the rock didn't sever the rein," remarked Rock Dog. "We'd never have found the shoe in the snow."

CHAPTER 32

Doctors of Archaeology

DURING THE WINTER, Ricardo described to his father the impact of the British Museum on both him and Rock Dog, and the following autumn the two enrolled at the University of Denver. Rock Dog pursued an undergraduate degree and Ricardo an advanced degree in archaeology. For the next five years, the two studied in Denver all winter and spent the summers on the southern Colorado rodeo circuit. Rock Dog turned out to be an incredible student and, by the end of that time, he was only a year behind Ricardo to qualify for a PhD in archaeology.

"Wait, wait, Great Grandfather," interrupted Juan. "What about rebuilding the horse herd?"

"Good question," replied the old man. "I forgot to cover that. While we were in England, Dad made several long trips to the Rodriguez hacienda to seek counsel on what to do with the large amount of money he'd received from the British for the horses. He had no experience with such things, but knew Senor Rodriguez had a strong financial background from his years in Mexico City. First, my father was advised to adopt a family name and he chose "Valdez". Next, after much consideration, they decided some of the money should be invested in new American businesses that reflected the changing world, rather than putting all of it back in the horse business. They chose Ford Motor Company and Standard Oil. The balance of the funds they divided between American and Swiss banks."

"We know about Ford trucks," Juan said. Their father had driven Ford pickups for years.

"Yes, of course," Great Grandfather smiled. "Let's just say both companies have been successful. The dividends they pay will take care of the family for many generations."

"But you live so simply," said Sophia. "You don't buy a lot of things. You make these beautiful pieces of furniture by hand and you sell vegetables to the community. It sounds like you are actually rich!"

"I do all those things," acknowledged their relative, "because I love the Valley; I love gardening; and I love making furniture. Rock Dog and I finished our archaeology work more than 25 years ago: no more remote places to explore, no more hair-raising adventures. We wanted to return to our families and heritage. Simple things enrich life; we don't need a lot of material possessions. I have plenty of money in the bank, but much of the income from the investments goes to help needy people all over the world. I know your dad and mom will follow this practice and I hope the two of you will also, when the money comes to you."

"I think I understand," replied Sophia. "There's nothing like evening fishing on the river, with ducks and geese flying overhead, or glassing the open parks with binoculars for elk in the fall and hearing them bugle, or seeing fresh snow flying as we snowmobile among the peaks in the winter. These are the things we talk about all the time. These are the things that mean a lot to us."

"Right," agreed Great Grandfather. "Rock Dog and I would be sitting in the middle of some blazing desert thinking about the clear water of the Rio Grande, or hunting in snow at timberline, planning to enter calf roping and team tying competitions when we got back. We cherished the experiences we grew up with."

"Hold on, Great Grandfather," interjected Juan. "Are you telling us you are *Doctor* Valdez? That you and *Doctor* Rock Dog traveled all over the world on archaeology projects? Why hasn't anyone told us about this?"

"First, he changed his name to Doggit as he advanced in the academic world," replied the old man. "There's a play on words there which we always laughed about, since we did a lot of bulldogging as young men. So his title became Dr. Doggit. No one outside of locals knew any different. And yes, we did travel to some rather incredible places, although East Africa was an area we concentrated on for years."

"But surely people in the San Luis Valley knew about you," Juan persisted. "You must be famous!"

"Not really," Great Grandfather smiled. "All they knew was we spent a lot of time up in Denver at the University; when we came home it was all about rodeo-ing, hunting, and fishing. We never talked much about our work because Dad still had the ranch and in those days it was pretty isolated so we didn't interact with a lot of people. Besides, folks weren't interested in archaeology; they were focused on farming and ranching."

"What's it like to be an archaeologist?" Sophia wanted to know.

"It's hard work, actually. One spends weeks digging and sifting dirt in remote, primitive areas to find artifacts, then months in laboratories or museums trying to interpret them."

"It must be exciting," she said.

"Sometimes," he acknowledged. "Like when Carter discovered the tomb of Tutankhamun in Egypt. But even that took months of careful work before the treasure was revealed. Most of the work isn't nearly so glamorous, just carefully piecing together small bits of information to gain a comprehensive view of a part of history, or perhaps a civilization. Sometimes it can be boring if you find nothing after weeks and weeks of work."

"Did you ever go to Peru?"

"Of course! The mystery of the medallion was paramount in my mind in those days. We went to Peru every year for at least 10 years and worked at a number of sites, including Machu Picchu, but none of them turned out to be Pattiti. The mountains are so vast and rugged; it was like trying to find a needle in a haystack, so we turned our attention to other places like Africa.

"East Africa. Why East Africa?" inquired Juan.

"Actually, Southeast Africa," said Great Grandfather. "The present country of Zimbabwe, because there was evidence of a surprising and fascinating Iron Age culture there."

CHAPTER 33

Grand Zimbabwe

"I CAN'T BELIEVE IT!" exclaimed Rock Dog, staring at the 36-foot high wall in front of them. "There's no mortar, just stones the size of bricks fitted closely together. How old do you think it is?"

"The Portuguese discovered it in the early 1530's and it was already a ruin," replied Ricardo, looking in awe at the towering construction. "This took a long time to build, and I'll bet it was here for at least 300 years before the Portuguese found it.."

"It's like the Inca ruins we studied," said the Ute, "but without the massive rocks; thousands of these stones had to be cut and shaped before they could construct a wall. It must have been an incredible undertaking." As they walked around the interior of the huge walled area, they noticed several new trenches along its edges and one alongside a conical stone tower rising 18 feet in the air.

"The excavations must be from the English expedition last year," remarked Ricardo. "They found artifacts that indicate this was the hub of a large trading area, but they didn't have time for extensive work. The reason the British Academy invited us to research the site is because of the evidence we uncovered about North American trade with the Inca Empire and also because we could spend six weeks here."

"Your family's oral history helped us uncover artifacts pointing to trade between North and South America and I think the British really liked our work," agreed the Ute.

It was late fall in 1929. The two had traveled by steamer to England to pay their respects at the British Academy for the invitation and collect the necessary approvals to reach the site. They boarded a ship crossing the Mediterranean and passing through the Suez Canal to the east coast of Africa. From there it was railroad and lorry (British flatbed truck) travel to the remote site. Outside the great enclosure, stone ruins covered hundreds of acres and they made camp beside a spring flowing out of a hillside. For the next month and a half the Americans, with 10 workers, dug trenches, sifted dirt through large pans with wire screens, and catalogued artifacts.

The only relief from the long hours of work came from morning or evening hunts for meat to supply the camp. Both men were excellent shots and, while in London, had acquired rifles suited for Africa. Two of the Shona workers were skilled trackers and put the Americans in range of game almost every outing. To the confusion of the English gunsmith, they had declined shotguns; Ricardo's sling was all they needed to provide a variety of fowl to supplement the fare. When the trackers showed the cook and other workers guinea fowl hit in the head while flying, the men were amazed.

Both Americans began to fall in love with Africa. They reveled in the chilly hunts at dawn as the rising sun revealed spectacular vistas. Scattered across the plains were vast herds of grazing zebra, impala, and wildebeest. Giraffe stretched graceful necks to browse on the tops of acacia trees and in the distance an elephant herd might be fording a river, their little ones all about their feet. At night, they sat in canvas chairs drinking coffee and watching the fire while the workers sang beautiful melodies around their own fire nearby, occasionally accompanied by the thunderous roars of lions in the hills. All too soon it was over. As they carefully packed wooden crates with items they'd found, Rock Dog looked around the campsite.

"I think we've found enough material that the British Academy will invite us back," he mused. "The iron hoes and gongs verify Iron Age activity here, and the pottery and gold beads could certainly point to a trading center. We need more time to dig; the area's so huge."

"If we get another invitation, we'll have to bring Martha and Gabby. This country is incredible; they'll love it!" exclaimed Ricardo.

"I was thinking exactly the same thing," replied the Ute.

CHAPTER 34
Martha

"WHOA, GREAT GRANDFATHER. Stop right there," interjected Sophia. "What's this about Martha and Gabby! You've never mentioned them before, or any women for that matter."

"Oh, they were our wives. Didn't I tell you about them?" said the old man with an innocent expression.

"You know very well you didn't," replied Sophia indignantly. She had always been interested in the romantic side of the family history and wasn't about to overlook any real or imagined "slips of memory" on her relative's part.

"It's very simple really; we'd both been married a year earlier, but Martha had contracted to conduct a six-week teaching seminar in Mexico City and Gabby's father had lost his top foreman, so we had to go alone that first trip," explained Great Grandfather. "Now, as we packed up artifacts..." he made as if to continue the story.

"No, no, no," Sophia was not about to be put off. "Who were they and how did you meet them? We want all the details."

"You've always said you want us to know everything about the family history," said Juan, stepping in to back up his sister.

"All right, all right," said Great Grandfather, throwing his hands in the air. "But I need another cup of coffee to get through this." With his back turned as he entered the house, neither of the twins could see the wide grin on his face. When he re-emerged, his face was serious, as though he were trying to remember details. "Now, let me see if I can get this right...," he began.

"Hah," snorted Sophia. "Your mind is like a steel trap! You just don't want to tell us about your love life!"

"If you insist," he said, taking a sip of coffee. "About two years before we went to Africa, I took my usual break from the local rodeos and caught the train to Santa Fe to spend a couple of weeks with Bruno. He was still my closest friend, other than Rock Dog, and we always got together during the summer in New

Mexico to fish the San Juan River, and during the fall in Colorado to hunt elk...."

As they drove to the ranch in a new two-seater Model T Ford convertible, Bruno mentioned that one of his cousins from Mexico City was visiting. "She's a history teacher," he said, "who's hardly ever been out of the city. She's had riding lessons, though, and is an excellent horsewoman. We didn't know how she'd react to the country, but she's been out with us almost every day this month checking cattle and exercising horses. Gissy just graduated from college in Spain and is home also; the two of them have become fast friends."

"I can't wait to see the family," said Ricardo. "So much has happened in the year since I was here."

"You know that Armando moved back to live with us?" asked Bruno. "He said that your father didn't have enough horses to keep him busy anymore, but I think the real reason was the cold winters in Colorado." They both laughed.

"That old man was one great rider," commented Ricardo. "But he never enjoyed the snow."

"He sits a horse straight as a ramrod even in his 70's," observed his friend.

The sun was low in the west as they pulled to a stop in front of the familiar house. The large front door flew open and Gissy raced down the walk to embrace Ricardo in a huge hug.

"Look at you," he said, holding her at arm's length. "You're all grown up, and you're beautiful."

"I've been grown up for quite some time," she sniffed. "You've just never noticed. Besides, I'm a college graduate now and I'm engaged to a man from Spain." She flashed a beautiful ring. "He's coming here next month."

"We're not sure what he's going to think of New Mexico," said Jorge Rodriguez, as the rest of the family followed Gissy down the walk. "She says his family raises cattle, but the climate there is a lot more lush than our deserts." He stepped back as Anna and Christa brushed past to greet Ricardo.

"My favorite student," beamed the older woman, her hair now liberally sprinkled with white. "The one who became Doctor Valdez!"

"I never would have made it without your teaching," said Ricardo. "Nor without your hospitality," he said to Anna, giving her a big hug.

"And this is Martha," said Gissy, as the others stepped aside for him to meet the woman who'd followed them to the car. She was dressed in boots, a long riding skirt, and white blouse. Around her slender waist was a leather belt decorated with silver conchos, and her long jet-black hair was secured with a wide red ribbon. Brown eyes stared at him from a stunning oval face and perfect white teeth flashed as she smiled a greeting.

"I've heard so much about you," she said, extending her hand. "According to Gissy, there's no finer horseman in the American West." Ricardo stood there flabbergasted; he had never seen a more beautiful woman!

"It's okay to shake her hand," said Gissy with a giggle. "She won't bite."

"Excuse me," he stammered, taking the hand gracefully held out to him. "It's just that I thought a teacher from the city would be…" He bit off the words before he got himself in more trouble.

"Would be what?" Gissy was having huge fun with his discomfort, while the others were trying hard not to laugh. "Plain and wrinkled, possibly hunched over with spectacles?"

"No, of course not," he flashed Bruno's sister a helpless look. "But when Bruno said she was from the city, I…" Once again he stopped in abject confusion. Christa stepped in to rescue him.

"Let's adjourn to the patio; I have some cold lemonade waiting and the dinner bell will ring before long." She led the way back toward the house. Inexplicably, Ricardo found himself walking beside Martha. Her head came just to his shoulder and she glanced up with laughing eyes.

"Surely you met a lot of female teachers during your studies," she said.

"Yes, of course," he replied, having recovered somewhat. "But most of them are so studious they don't do anything out of the ordinary. Coming to the hacienda and riding with the men every day is not what I'd consider normal activity for a city teacher."

"Didn't Bruno tell you I have an advanced degree, for which I studied the history of great horse cultures around the world?" Ricardo stopped to stare at her.

"I had no idea. Horses and my history are strongly intertwined. My family was in the business of raising and training horses for 300 years not far from here. My mother died giving birth to me and my father had me on horseback at two. I came to the hacienda with him to demonstrate horses when I was five."

"I know all about that," she said. "The finest war horses and buffalo runners in the entire Southwest came from the canyon where demons protected herds and trainers alike. The integrity and honor of the family that lived there is renowned and the young boy who helped deliver horses to my uncle demonstrated riding skills the vaqueros couldn't match. The history of your family is exactly the kind of thing I study and teach. My classroom is mostly riding arenas," she added. "Do you still ride bareback?"

"It depends on the horse," he said, glad for the opportunity to get into a familiar topic with this remarkable woman. "If it's one of our horses, I just use a small pad. They are so responsive to body cues that bareback works best. If the horse belongs to someone else, I generally use a very small, light saddle, which I've modified from the English version. For rodeos, or for working cattle, I use a light Western saddle because I want a horn to dally on. (Dally means to take a quick wrap around the horn with the rope so that the horse is holding the weight of the roped animal.)"

"I'd like to see you demonstrate on one of the Rodriguez' horses," she ventured.

"We'll see whether Bruno has retained any of the training techniques we taught him years ago," Ricardo said in a loud voice to catch the ear of his friend, who was discreetly walking several steps in front of them.

"Don't know if we've ever had better trained horses than the ones we're working with now," retorted Bruno over his shoulder.

CHAPTER 35

Gabby

SUPPER IN THE BIG dining hall was a raucous affair that night as vaqueros and their families welcomed Ricardo back. He was a great favorite with everyone and children of all ages begged for stories of far-away places when dinner was finished. The women also noted that Gissy had moved from her accustomed place beside Martha to a seat across the table and Anna had seated Ricardo beside the teacher. A veranda had been added to the dining hall and everyone moved outside with coffee to enjoy the desert evening. Standing at the rail with Gissy, Martha watched the lean cowboy from Colorado sitting in a rocking chair telling stories to nearly two-dozen kids seated around him on the floor.

"He does this every night he's here," whispered Gissy. "They never get tired of it, even if he tells the same tale a few times. The older ones will prompt him for stories from last year or the year before."

"Mmmm," murmured the teacher, unable to take her eyes off the handsome face.

"Uh-oh, he's got you hooked now too," giggled the younger woman.

And so he had. For the next two weeks Martha and Ricardo were inseparable, riding every day, taking walks under the large cottonwoods now shading the stream, talking with Christa and Anna on the patio. Whether it was working cattle with Jorge and Bruno, or training horses for the vaqueros, one was never far from the other. At the end of two weeks, Ricardo wired his father and Rock Dog that he would be staying another two weeks and would miss the next couple of rodeos. By the time Martha had to return to Mexico City, plans had been made for Ricardo to spend Christmas with her family.

September colors were in full glory when Ricardo swung off the train in Alamosa. Rock Dog was there to meet him, accompanied by a very pretty woman in a long colorful dress. The Ute introduced her as Gabby and said she came from a ranch near Taos.

"You know Jose Martinez, who married my sister Butterfly?" asked the Indian.

"How could I forget him?" groused his friend. "We've never been able to beat him in calf roping."

"We've got more trouble now," said Rock Dog, "because Jose introduced his best friend, Manuel, to the rodeo circuit this summer. Manuel hasn't lost a roping competition yet."

"If that's the case, I'm glad I got detained in Santa Fe."

"Yeah, I heard about your "detention;" she sounds wonderful," grinned the Ute. "Anyway, Gabby is Manuel's sister and ropes as well as he does!"

"It sounds like we need to get her on our side," said Ricardo, staring at the girl in admiration.

"That's what I'm trying to do," exclaimed Rock Dog. "We spent a lot of time together at rodeos this summer and now she's here spending time with my family while I help your father with some horses before classes start in Denver. By the way, the University has received a batch of trade artifacts for us to study and wants us to teach a couple of classes about the Inca. Also, I've asked Gabby to marry me after the school year's over."

"And…?" Ricardo stared at the girl with raised eyebrows.

"I've accepted, of course," laughed Gabby. "I've never met anyone as wonderful as this fascinating man!"

"You realize you'll become Mrs. Doggit?" questioned Dr. Valdez, feigning a frown.

"Yes, and it's a perfect name because Manuel has never been any good at bulldogging," she chuckled, as she linked arms with both men and headed for the truck.

During Christmas vacation, a telegram to Rock Dog said it all:

```
You and Gabby are invited to our
wedding in Mexico City next July.
```

CHAPTER 36

Danger in the Dark

TRUE TO RICARDO'S PREDICTION, Martha and Gabby fell in love with Africa when they accompanied their husbands on the second trip to Grand Zimbabwe. The men added three large wall tents, an expanded camp staff, cots, chairs, and tables to the expedition, resulting in a trio of heavily loaded lorries arriving at the dig site one afternoon. In short order, a comfortable camp was established beside the same stream they had used two years earlier and the archaeologists were giving their wives a tour of the ruins.

That evening after supper, the four sat at their camp table watching sparks rise from the campfire and listening to the men singing nearby. Behind them two of the big white tents glowed golden from lanterns within, but beyond the fire it was pitch black.

"I can't believe how quickly night fell," remarked Martha.

"And cooled things off," added Gabby. "I'd never have believed we'd welcome these heavy sweaters after the heat of the day." Ricardo was about to comment on how they would welcome even more the warm sleeping bags when three lions began roaring out in the dark. The noise was so loud, and sounded so close, that both women leaped to their feet and stared wildly about.

"Are they coming into camp?" whispered Martha, moving to stand beside her husband's chair. He grabbed her hand reassuringly.

"In all fairness, they actually may come through camp while we're sleeping," he said. "But right now they're out in the hills somewhere, just making noise."

"If I had to protect you, it might be a bit difficult this way," chuckled Rock Dog finding Gabby on his lap. "It is unnerving the first time you hear it," he added, giving her a hug.

"I thought they were going to pounce right on us," she exclaimed in a shaky voice.

"They're actually some distance away," said her husband. "But the first time we heard them at night, I had a shell in the chamber and the safety off my rifle so fast I didn't remember doing it!" The roars diminished as the lions moved away and quiet descended on the camp.

"The men are still singing," marveled Gabby. "I wonder if they saw our reaction?"

"Almost certainly," replied Ricardo. "They probably got a big kick out of it, but they understand how scary it is the first time."

"Wait until they see the two of you shoot," said Rock Dog. "They'll have nothing but respect." Gabby had been shooting her entire life on the ranch, but Martha had had no such training. Since moving to Del Norte, however, she had spent countless hours with Gabby learning to shoot; her marksmanship was now almost equal to that of the Taos girl. Armed with rifles from the English gunsmith, the two were anxious to join their husbands in providing food for the camp. Indeed, after a few days, the Shona trackers reported to the crew that American women were excellent hunters.

As Ricardo had predicted, from time to time pugmarks appeared in the dirt around camp but nothing was disturbed. Regular food was kept in large metal boxes and game was butchered in the bush, where hyena quickly consumed the leavings, so the lions were deemed to be passing through on their way elsewhere. A month later that changed.

"What are you doing?" asked Martha sleepily, awakened by the click of a rifle bolt ramming a shell into the firing chamber.

"Shhhh, there's something outside the tent," whispered Ricardo, moving to stand close to her. "See if you can get the lantern lit." In an instant, she was wide-awake fumbling for matches and the lantern on the table between their cots. Fortunately, she found both instantly and light flared against the white canvas walls and ceiling.

"Turn it up full," he urged in a low voice, as the far wall of the tent swayed slightly. Ricardo swung to face the wall, rifle against his shoulder, aimed at the canvas. "Get behind me," he breathed, straining to hear any sound outside. Martha stepped to his back.

"Do you want me to get my rifle?" she whispered.

"There's no time. Put your hands on my hips and stay directly behind me. If it comes, I'm only going to have time for one shot." She realized he was positioning her not only to be out of the line of his fire, but also to fall underneath him if whatever it was couldn't be stopped. Utter silence reigned as Ricardo, medallion red hot against his skin, turned slowly in a circle trying to locate the danger. The hair on his arms was standing up and he knew that a deadly menace lurked on the other side of the thin canvas.

A minute ticked by...then another...

Martha was trembling as she pivoted behind Ricardo, hands lightly on his hips. The silence was infinitely more terrifying because there was nothing to identify what might be outside. The grunt of a leopard, or cry of a hyena, would at least let them know what they were dealing with. The rifle barrel in Ricardo's hands was as steady as a rock and she knew he was totally focused on repelling whatever was threatening them. She swung her head from side to side, sweeping the tent walls with her eyes to spot any movement.

"Look out, the front flaps!" Martha suddenly cried in her husband's ear as she caught a slight movement in the corner of her eye. At that instant Ricardo was facing the rear of the tent. He spun like lightning, Martha lunging desperately to stay behind him, as the canvas flaps started to bow inward, and pulled the trigger. In his haste, the shot went high and he worked the bolt as fast as he could to load another shell, crouching slightly, his eyes on the entrance. The noise of the rifle in the tent was deafening, but the hyper vigilant couple hardly noticed it as they stared at the loosely tied flaps, waiting for the attack. It never came…the canvas swayed slightly, then hung motionless.

"I think it's gone," murmured Ricardo. "Are you okay?"

"Scared to death, but otherwise fine," she answered with a tiny laugh. There was a shout from the adjacent tent.

"Ricardo, are you alright?"

"Yes, but get your rifle and a lantern," he called. "I think a lion was stalking us!" Noise from the workers' camp indicated they had been wakened by the shot and Martha saw light flicker through the canvas as their fire flamed up.

"Bwana, are you safe?" yelled one of the trackers.

"Yes, be careful!" yelled Ricardo, rifle still to his shoulder. "Watch for a lion."

"There's nothing here now," said the man, approaching the tents holding a large flaming branch. There was a "snick" as Ricardo slipped on the safety of his weapon. He turned and hugged his wife.

"Let's go see what was menacing us."

"What woke you?" she asked, shrugging into a heavy jacket.

"The medallion: it was nearly burning my chest," he explained, reaching for the tent straps.

CHAPTER 37
Tracks

THE GROUND REVEALED the story as clearly to
the tracker, Joseph, as if he had observed the whole
incident.

"See here," he commented in the light of several
lanterns. "It approached the rear of your tent in a crawl,
very slowly. Something must have startled it because
the tracks back away and move to the side before closing in again."

"It may have moved when I leaped out of bed and
loaded the rifle," observed Ricardo.

"Probably," said the Shona hunter. "But it wasn't
scared off and moved along the side of the tent before
jumping away once more."

"Maybe when I lit the lantern," said Martha.

"Yes," agreed Joseph. "It came to the front flaps prepared to spring. See how the tracks of the back legs are dug into the ground? The right paw was raised to the tent and replaced…see how this track slightly overlaps the original one?"

"That's when my wife saw the flaps move," offered Ricardo.

"You were seconds away from an attack," said the tracker. "Those ties on the flaps wouldn't have held and it would have been on you in an instant." Martha shuddered at the thought.

"The rifle shot stopped it," mused Rock Dog. "Good thinking, my friend."

"There was no thinking involved," said Ricardo, "I was facing the wrong direction when Martha saw the canvas move and fired before I was ready."

"Just as well," replied the Ute. "You scared it off."

"But Joseph, we've had lions through the camp regularly," said Gabby. "Why did this one want to attack?" The tracker again walked slowly around the tent, holding a lantern close to the ground.

"I think it's an injured lioness," observed Joseph finally, "the tracks are smaller than that of a male. See how the right back paw is twisted to the outside and drags at every step? She's been shot or wounded in a trap. When any big cat is prevented from catching its normal prey, it often turns to humans. They are the easiest of all animals to kill." The Americans stared at him in silence at this candid observation.

"Will she come back?" said Martha, voicing the question on all their minds.

"I think so," answered Joseph. "The females are the hunters and she won't give up until she has food. We'll have to keep fires burning at night."

"Let's begin right now," exclaimed Rock Dog, heading toward the woodpile with his lantern. In short order, flames were leaping up from both fires and a schedule was established among the men to keep them burning.

Back in their tent, Martha twisted about on her cot, unable to sleep.

"Are you awake?" she murmured.

"Yes," came the answer. "I've been wondering whether you'd be able to get back to sleep."

"I keep seeing the flaps move," she said. "It was one of the scariest moments of my life."

"Let's go sit by the fire," Ricardo suggested. "I think there's still some coffee left over from supper." Dawn found them asleep in comfortable camp chairs, side by side in front of the fire. They were holding hands, but Ricardo's rifle was lying across his knees.

CHAPTER 38

Maneater

Two days later a man walked into camp as the couples finished breakfast, deep in conversation about the ancient shards they'd uncovered the day before with what appeared to be Chinese markings. They were imagining the excitement in England over such a find. It could confirm what had previously been pure speculation: that trade among ancient peoples was far more extensive than the modern world imagined.

The stranger stood quietly near the table. His only clothing was a loose robe looped under his right arm, and tied atop his left shoulder; he carried a short bow and a quiver with three arrows at his hip. He had approached so silently that it was several minutes before

Ricardo noticed him and voiced a greeting in Swahili. The answer was unintelligible, so the archeologist went and brought Joseph over from the workers' tent. There ensued a rapid conversation between tracker and visitor in a dialect that the Americans had never heard. Finally, Joseph turned toward the table.

"He's from a village five miles from here. Last night, a lion got through the boma and dragged off a young man, without waking anyone. They tracked it to a group of rocky hills nearby, but the undergrowth was so dense they didn't dare go further. They are requesting that you come and kill the man-eater."

"We saw bomas around every village on the way here and you told us that all the livestock and people are shut inside once it gets dark," remarked Martha. "The boma walls must have been seven feet high and made from brush with long, needle-sharp thorns; I don't see how any predator could get through!"

"A normal lion or leopard will rarely attempt it," replied Joseph, "but a desperate man-eater has cunning beyond our understanding. If it gets through the barrier once, no one is safe in that village again."

"How could it possibly take a man away without waking anyone?" asked Gabby. "Surely his screams would have alerted people?"

"My guess is that he was bitten through the skull and died instantly," answered the tracker. "It seems impossible that a lion could get through a boma, enter a hut, kill a man, and drag him away without attracting attention, but this is not the first time it's happened."

"We've got to help those people," said Rock Dog, rising from the table. "I'll get my rifle."

"So will I," muttered Ricardo, following suit. "If it's the same lion that came here, we've got a score to settle."

"Grab your rifle," said Gabby to Martha. "We're going with them."

"My thought exactly," replied the Mexican woman, pushing back from the table.

"Whoa, whoa!" cried Ricardo. "What do you think you're doing? You can't come with us; it's too dangerous." But both women had disappeared into their tents. When they emerged, rifles in hand, Martha spoke before he could open his mouth.

"If you think the two of you are going off without us, you've got another thought coming," she announced in a tone that brooked no nonsense. "We are excellent shots and if you need to separate, each of you will need back-up." She had rehearsed this little speech on her way in and out of the tent and it was accompanied by flashing eyes.

"But, but…," stammered her husband, at a loss for words.

"She kind of makes sense, don't you think," suggested the Ute, suppressing a smile. "You never can tell when we might have to split up." He loved the spunk of these women and knew they weren't going to be denied.

"I suppose," grumbled Ricardo, realizing he was hopelessly outnumbered. "But if Joseph says the brush is too dangerous, the two of you will have to stay out." The two women nodded solemnly and the tracker averted his face. He knew that both wives would follow their husbands into danger no matter what he said. He directed the couples to bring warm clothes and hurried off to have the cook prepare sandwiches and thermoses of hot tea. Within an hour they were bumping their way slowly across the veldt in one of the lorries.

CHAPTER 39

Spoor

It was mid-afternoon when the lorry bounced down a long, grassy slope through grazing cattle guarded by several boys and approached a village of nine huts, surrounded by an impressive fence of thorn brush. The huts were circular, constructed of mud walls and conical straw roofs, a gap in the boma acting as a gate. Chickens and goats meandered about—at night all the animals would be herded inside and brush pulled across the opening.

The trip had been lengthened by a detour to ford a small river and the new arrivals were chafing to get on the lion's trail. Their guide jumped from the vehicle and entered the village, returning shortly with several men led by a gray-haired individual who was apparently the leader. In his hand was a bloodstained remnant of cloth to which he pointed as he and Joseph talked. After a few minutes, the men started walking on the outside of the boma toward the far side of the village.

"He wants to show us where the lion escaped," explained the tracker as he beckoned the group to join them. "They found the shred of cloth and one hand about halfway to those hills." He pointed at a long ridgeline two miles away.

"Are there tracks to follow?" asked Rock Dog, shaken by the reality of the situation.

"Yes," replied Joseph. Nearly opposite the entrance, the elder stopped and pointed to the ground. In the dirt were pugmarks and drag marks stretching away toward the distant hills.

"Let's use the lorry,' suggested Ricardo, heading back to the truck. "We can save time since these men have already worked out the trail."

"I'll wait here," said Joseph. "I want to study the tracks." When Ricardo drove up, the Shona tracker looked grim. "It's the same lioness that tried to get into your tent," he announced. "She has a twisted back paw that drags at every step."

The lorry had no doors, so it was easy for one of the villagers to stand on the running board beside Ricardo and point the way. The others rode on the flat-bed with four workers who had come along from the dig. A mile from the village, they came to a large dark stain on the ground and scattered bones.

"This is where she fed," explained Joseph. "Scavengers made short work of whatever was left." The four Americans were startled at his matter-of-fact tone. The ghastly scene was completely out of their frame of reference. Such things just didn't happen at home.

"How old was he?" asked Gabby from the back seat. After a short conversation with the leader, Joseph turned to her.

"Eighteen years old, he was the chief's son," Gabby's eyes filled with tears as she looked at the gray-haired man.

"Tell him his son will be avenged," she declared grimly.

The sun was low in the west when they reached the base of the ridge. Rising 300 feet, the gentle slope was covered with a jumble of large boulders and thick brush.

"I can see why these men didn't want to go further," exclaimed Ricardo as their guide pointed to a tunnel-like opening in the brush into which the tracks led. "That's hands-and-knees ground, and it's dark in there!" Indeed, the thicket was so dense one couldn't make out anything farther than 10 feet inside. He glanced at the sky. "There's only an hour or so of daylight left and we absolutely don't want to be caught in there after sunset. I suggest we camp on the hill above the village and come back first thing in the morning." Everyone nodded in agreement.

After dropping the villagers at the boma, the archaeologists and workers made camp on the knob above the village. Everyone collected wood until they had enough to last the night and then built a couple of large fires, a few yards apart. Teams of two were chosen to keep the flames going and watch for danger while the others stretched out on the ground between the fires. With the patch of blood-stained ground fresh in their minds, no one had trouble staying awake during their watch. The night passed uneventfully.

CHAPTER 40
Ambush

Magnified by dust in the atmosphere the sun was an enormous orange orb as it rose above the eastern horizon, highlighting the lorry was bumping along yesterday's trail. This time, the hunters were unaccompanied by villagers.

"They're confident we will rid them of the man-eater," explained Joseph, "so there's nothing for them to do out here."

"I wish we could be so sure," said Ricardo. "Who knows if the lion is even still around?"

"I also thought of that," answered the tracker. "I think some of us should make a wide circle and search the top of the ridge for tracks. If she went down the other side, we can start tracking her from there. If we find no pugmarks, she's probably still in the rocks and brush."

"Gabby and I'll go with you," said Rock Dog. "We can take two of the men for extra eyes and leave two to watch the hillside with Ricardo and Martha." By the time they reached the edge of the brush it was already hot. Rock Dog and the others took the lorry a quarter mile farther along the base of the hill, to where the brush and boulders gave way to a broad swath of grass stretching to the hilltop. Able to spot an attack in the grass, they made their way quickly to the ridgeline and started slowly back in the direction of their friends, studying the ground for tracks.

Ricardo, Martha, and the two men studied the hill before them. The archaeologist and his wife were using binoculars, but it was the sharp eyes of the worker named Peter that spotted movement.

"There!" he suddenly cried, pointing at a large rock 50 yards up the hill.

"What?" questioned Ricardo urgently.

"I saw something move beside that rock," the man said in a lower voice. "The one that's split on top." After Ricardo identified the boulder, he and Martha studied it closely through their binoculars, but could see nothing in the heavy brush. Minutes went by, in tense silence broken only by the buzzing of a fly.

"There," whispered the other worker excitedly, pointing downhill from the boulder. "The top of a branch moved slightly!"

"Are you sure?" asked Ricardo, but before the man could answer he knew it was true…the medallion had begun to warm. They were 15 yards from the opening in the brush, but he knew even a crippled animal could cover the distance quickly. "Let's move back a ways," he said. "Over by that anthill." Forty feet behind them, a six-foot anthill rose above the long grass. It was big enough that one of the men could climb on top and have a better view of the brushy hillside.

"Look," hissed Martha," I saw something tan move just uphill from the opening in the brush!" Simultaneously, she and her husband worked the bolts of their rifles, putting shells into the firing chambers, and both slipped the safety off. They backed slowly toward the anthill, weapons raised and ready to be snapped into firing position.

"Peter, can you climb up the mound and tell us if you see anything?" asked Ricardo, both husband and wife poised to shoot. They became aware that the birds and insects had gone silent, a sure sign that a large predator was close. Ricardo's voice was calm, belying the fact that the piece of silver had grown hot; he expected a charge at any second. The Shona worker placed a hand on each side of the hardened dirt and shinnied to the top of the mound in an instant.

"Nothing, Sir," he replied and then gave a great laugh. "Except that little dik-dik (small rock antelope) that just came out of the brush tunnel!" As he stood up to guffaw, Peter's foot slipped and he tumbled backwards off the anthill with a startled cry. At the sound, Martha swung around to see if he was hurt.

"Ricardo! Behind you!" She screamed, as she caught sight of a tawny form flashing through the tall grass. Her husband spun around as a gun roared in his ear. He just had time to take in a kaleidoscope of waving stalks and snarling head with flattened ears when the rifle roared again and he was struck in the chest by a hurtling body that drove him five feet backwards onto the hard ground. All went black…

"There's just a small puncture wound on his chest, Memsaab, I think he hit his head on a rock," Peter's voice came dimly. Ricardo became aware of a splitting headache as he forced his eyes open and saw his wife's face hovering above his. She had a stricken look and he tried to give her a reassuring smile. Her eyes flew wide.

"Oh sweetheart, I thought you were dead!" she wailed. "The lion was in the tall grass behind us the whole time. If Peter hadn't fallen off the anthill she would have killed you!" He struggled to sit up, but became so dizzy he let her pull his head back onto her lap.

"Well, I'm not dead and I don't think anything's broken," he croaked in an attempt to lighten the situation. "But my chest hurts and I have an awful headache."

"She got a claw into you, but your wife's quick shots were fatal; the lioness was dead by the time she struck you." It was Peter's voice again. "We had to cut your shirt apart for a bandage." Ricardo glanced down and saw a strip of khaki colored cloth wrapped across his bare chest, the now cool medallion draped to one side. Martha held a canteen to his mouth.

"Take some water," she urged. Several swallows of the cool liquid had an amazing effect.

"I'm all right now," he said, struggling to a sitting position. The first thing he noticed was blood all over his pants. Seeing his stare, Martha put a hand on his shoulder.

"We thought the blood was yours," she explained, "but it's from the lion." A few feet away lay the big cat, fearsome teeth bared in a bloody snarl, great claws still extended from the front paws. "We had to drag her off you," she added. Ricardo forced himself to his feet, supported by her arm around his waist and waited for his head to clear.

"I knew the man-eater was close because of the medallion," he said. "But I thought it was in the brush facing us. I was waiting for a glimpse of it to shoot, never dreaming it could be behind us." He stared at her. "How did you do it?"

"I really don't know," answered Martha in a low voice. "It all happened so fast." John, the second worker, spoke up.

"Sir, I witnessed it. When Peter fell, I turned and saw the charging lion at the same time as Memsaab. She snapped the rifle up and fired once when it was 20 feet away. Her second shot was point blank into its neck as it sprang. One claw raked you, but the beast was already dead."

Back in their camp at Grand Zimbabwe that night, the two couples sat in camp chairs before the fire, millions of stars blazing in the sky above. The village chief had insisted they stay for a large celebration feast and it was after dark when they finally reached their camp.

"That was remarkable shooting," mused Rock Dog. "The first bullet was directly in the lion's face and absolutely fatal, but the animal's vitality was such that she was still able to spring for the kill. The second bullet knocked her off target so the claw struck Ricardo's chest instead of his face. The amazing thing is the timing: I've been shooting all my life and don't think I could have worked the bolt of a rifle to get off two shots that fast." For a moment all were silent, staring at the burning logs.

"I give Gabby the credit," Martha finally said with a small laugh. "Hundreds of hours of training, along with our actual hunting experiences, must have changed this city girl into a shooter."

"So it did," agreed Ricardo, gazing at his beautiful wife, "so it did!"

CHAPTER 41

Retirement

"**N**O WAY!" EXCLAIMED JUAN. "Our great grand-mother saved you from a man-eating lion? How come we've never heard about this?" The old man regarded him with a grin.

"Well, perhaps it's because you've kept me busy with the more ancient history of the medallion for the past two years."

"Great Grandfather, are you teasing us?" Sophia jumped in. "You literally had a dead man-eating lion on top of you and you were covered with its blood?"

"Literally," answered their relative. "Don't you believe me?"

"Of course, we believe everything you tell us, but all of this is so weird. We never even knew you were an archeologist," the girl explained.

"Do you want proof about the lion?" he asked. Neither twin spoke, out of respect for their elder, but he could see affirmations in their eyes. Unbuttoning his blue work shirt, he pulled it open, exposing the right side of his chest. Etched in the brown skin above his heart was a wicked looking curved scar, six inches long.

"She really got you, didn't she?" breathed Juan.

"Yes she did, and it would have been a lot worse except for your great grandmother."

"She actually spent all those hours with Gabby shooting?" asked Sophia.

"Absolutely," replied Great Grandfather. "She had already come to love the hacienda life when she met me, and Gabby explained what it would be like to marry a man who loved to hunt and fish. The two of them were like peas in a pod and Martha was determined to excel in everything Gabby could teach her."

"Did they always go with you on digs?" asked the girl.

"The four of us traveled together all over the world for some years, until children came along. After that, Rock Dog and I cut back on the digs and turned to lecturing so we could be close to our families. Finally, we retired to the Valley."

"What happened then?" inquired Juan.

"We all lived in Del Norte for a while. In their mid-70's, Martha and Gabby died peacefully within a few days of each other." The old man's eyes filled with tears and he stared at the distant peaks. After a few minutes, he continued. "Rock Dog and I couldn't stay in Del Norte—not with all the memories—so we moved to Center. He died quietly in his sleep a few years later and I began the gardening business to keep myself busy until it was time to pass on the medallion."

"We've had it for two years and you're stronger than ever," ventured Juan. "I don't mean any disrespect, but shouldn't you be feeling the effects of aging now that you're not wearing it?"

"I've thought about that very thing," acknowledged Great Grandfather. "I believe it may have something to do with what you observed at the Solstice."

"The stonemason?"

"Not the man himself, but what he was doing. I've told you all along that I think the two of you are destined to uncover the secret of the medallion, but perhaps it involves all three of us."

CHAPTER 42

News Flash

"WE CAME AS SOON AS you called," Juan said, as the door of the trim white house opened. It was ten days later and their relative had phoned during supper to say he needed to see them as soon as possible. Not waiting for dessert, the twins sprinted the two blocks to Great Grandfather's house. "Is everything alright?"

"I couldn't be better," replied the old man, closing the door behind them. "I want to show you something I recorded yesterday." After they were seated in the living room, he poked a remote and his flat-screen TV sprang to life. A well-known broadcaster stared at them.

"We take you now to Peru, where an exciting discovery has just been made," she announced. The scene shifted to a reporter with a microphone standing in sunlight outside the entryway of a brown building.

"I'm here at the National Museum of Archaeology, Anthropology, and History in Lima, Peru," said the young woman. "Today the Museum announced an important discovery in the Andes Mountains." She turned to a bearded man standing beside her. "This is Jose Mendez from the Museum. Can you tell us about the discovery?"

"Certainly," he replied. "A party of climbers was in an extremely remote, high mountain valley when they came across an inscribed fragment of rock lying at the edge of a boulder field. It was too big to carry out but they took pictures." He held an eight by ten black and white photograph toward the camera. "As you can see, it seems to show rays descending from the sun onto a mountain. There is a badly worn image carved at the base of the mountain." He pointed toward the bottom of the photograph. "It's small, but you can make out the circle, with symbols too eroded to decipher on its perimeter and a square in the middle."

"What do you think it means?" asked the reporter.

"We don't know, of course," answered Mendez, "but there are legends of a lost city in the Andes, named Pattiti, which was destroyed by its inhabitants after they killed an invading party of conquistadors. The legends have persisted for hundreds of years, but until now nothing has been found to substantiate them."

"Why do you think this one piece of rock might be a clue to the lost city?" questioned the reporter. "The climbers reported seeing no other artifacts."

"That's a good question. The sunbeams indicate that the mountain was an important place and the valley where the fragment was observed is on the flanks of a mountain. Legends say the city was well hidden and remote; it took more than 10 years for the conquistadors to find it. This location fits that description: it's nearly 3,000 meters, or 15,000 feet, high and so isolated we've no evidence that anyone in modern times has been there. It's also hemmed in by a tall ridge to the north and steep terrain on all other sides. This would have been an ideal setting in which to hide a city; however, aerial photographs reveal no evidence of an Inca road for miles and miles, which is confusing. The Inca had an extensive road system throughout the Empire and every city was accessed by one. So the lack of a road argues against a city, but even if the site is only that of a sacred temple, it would be a wonderful find. We will obviously learn more when a trained team gets up there."

"When will that be?"

"We should have an expedition at the site in less than 30 days."

"So there you have it," said the reporter, turning back toward the camera. "A group of archaeologists is gathering right now to explore the area. The terrain is so rough that they will have to hike at least four

days on foot from the closest road. Back to you..."
The scene changed to the American studio and Great
Grandfather turned the TV off. The twins stared at
him in stunned silence.

"It's a carving of the medallion on the stone; I'm
certain of it!" cried Juan. "You can't make out the
markings, but it's circular with a square in the middle."
Their relative nodded.

"But there's more!" exclaimed Sophia excitedly.
"The curator said there is a high ridge to the north.
Adzul climbed a ridge when he fled the city. Remember
the stones he rolled down on the conquistadors?" Great
Grandfather nodded again.

"Yes," Juan chimed in, "and he said aerial images
showed no Inca roads for miles. Qist had the roads
destroyed so the conquistadors couldn't find Pattiti.
It's got to be the site!" It was the old man's turn to stare.

"When does school start?" he asked.

"Two and a half weeks," replied Sophia. "Why?"

"I called a man in Lima whose father I knew," said
Great Grandfather. "He's approved visas and all the
government permits necessary for us to visit the site
as soon as we can get there. I hope I can get you back
in time for school because I know the coach wants
Juan there for football practice," he added with a grin.

"Don't we need passports?" stammered Sophia.

"I keep mine up to date. I had your mother scan
pictures of you and overnight the other necessary

documents. The visas and passports will be ready in Denver the day after tomorrow. We fly out that night, so you may want to go home and start packing."

"Wait a minute," said Juan in disbelief. "How could you possibly put all this together so fast?"

"Well, the passports were a bit expensive, I admit," acknowledged the old man. But Juan wasn't satisfied.

"The man in Peru, how could he get visas and approvals?"

"Oh, that," Great Grandfather said with a familiar twinkle in his eye. "When I made trips to Peru as an archeologist, I became great friends with his father because of our mutual Inca background. He was interested in the story of the medallion, cloth armor, and use of the sling. I knew all his children and after he died I maintained a friendship with his only son."

"This man must be in the government," guessed Juan.

"You might say so," smiled their relative. "My friend was President of the country and his son is the current Prime Minister.

CHAPTER 43

Lima

IT WAS LATE EVENING WHEN the big jet touched
down at Jorge Chavez International Airport in Lima,
Peru. The six-and-a-half-hour flight from Houston had
sped by with the excitement of comfort, wonderful food,
and movies, which their Business Class seats provided.
But perhaps the greatest surprise had come as Great
Grandfather appeared in the lobby of the Denver hotel
when they left for the airport. Gone were the jeans,
plaid shirt, and work boots he always wore. In their
place were tan slacks, a blue button-down shirt with
red-patterned tie, and a blue blazer. On his feet were
impeccable brown loafers. This was an image they'd
never imagined before.

"You know, I spent many years lecturing and presenting at meetings around the world," he explained almost apologetically as they both stared, openmouthed. "One has to dress properly for all sorts of occasions and, after all, we are going to meet the Prime Minister of Peru." They nodded dumbly, recalling the whirlwind shopping tour they'd made the day before with him and their mother. Their new suitcases held dressy clothes they'd never dreamed of wearing.

Upon presenting their passports to the customs official, the three were shown to a special line where they were whisked through into the general airport. At the baggage claim area, a man in a black suit, white shirt, and black tie was standing holding a printed sign reading "Valdez party," against his chest. He shook hands with Great Grandfather and helped carry their luggage to a Mercedes limousine waiting at the curb outside.

"The Prime Minister has gone overboard," their relative explained as the man slipped behind the wheel. "This is his personal car and driver. I expected to take a taxi to the hotel." Juan and Sophia were too awestruck by the luxurious vehicle to reply. It was past midnight and traffic was light as they sped through the streets and soon arrived at the Country Club Lima Hotel. The beautiful white two-story edifice they pulled up to eclipsed the limo experience. A curved driveway led to the brightly lit entrance, over which an ornate roof was supported by white columns. Two bellmen hurried down the steps to open the car doors and retrieve bags from the trunk. Inside, marble floors and elegant furniture graced the lobby, and beautiful chandeliers hung from a ceiling crossed by wood beams. The twins glanced around surreptitiously, trying not to reveal their astonishment.

"Good evening, Mr. Valdez. It's been many years since we've had the pleasure of your company," said the pleasant young woman behind the registration counter.

"You must have been barely born the last time I was here," said Great Grandfather with a smile. "Does the hotel keep records that far back?"

"Yes, sir; it's all computerized now of course."

"The property is just as beautiful as I remember," complimented the old man.

"Thank you, sir," she replied. "We have three connected rooms overlooking the gardens, as you requested."

"Wonderful!" exclaimed Great Grandfather. "Thank you; we've had a long day of travel."

"Have a pleasant stay," she said. "Breakfast is served in the dining room until 10:00 AM."

The large rooms each had a king size bed, desk, armchairs, large TV, and a magnificent tiled bathroom with separate shower and tub. Sophia had the middle room, but she and Juan kept running back through the connecting door to compare amenities, until Great

Grandfather appeared to gently suggest they get some sleep.

"I know how wonderful it all is," he said, "but we will have a busy day tomorrow getting ready for the trek." Despite all their excitement, their heads had scarcely hit their pillows before they were asleep.

The next day was filled with trips to the Museum and government offices to obtain written permission for visiting the site. Fortunately, the Prime Minister's office had already notified officials that the archaeologist and two teenagers were approved to proceed into the mountains. Great Grandfather rented a Land Rover and purchased tents, packs, and a mountain of food to supply them for the trip. He also arranged for llamas to meet them at the trailhead. As they transferred belongings into their new packs, Sophia happened to notice Great Grandfather carefully tucking an oddly-shaped leather parcel among his clothes, but in the excitement of getting ready she thought nothing of it. That evening they had dinner at the Nanka Restaurant with the Prime Minister and his wife.

"My father used to invite this wonderful man to our house to demonstrate the sling," said the handsome gray-haired official, gesturing at Great Grandfather. "I remember he could hit a grape hanging from a branch on the other side of the garden." He smiled, "My sisters and I always thought there must be some trick because we could never see the rock fly through the air; it was too fast."

"The first time he showed us the sling, he buried a rock in a tree across the street," said Juan. "I had to dig it out with my knife." They all laughed.

"Do you still make armor shirts?" inquired the Prime Minister. "I remember one demonstration where my father asked me to stab Ricardo with a knife. When I refused, for fear that I would hurt him, Father took the knife and struck, but nothing happened."

"Yes," replied Sophia, "Great Grandfather made one for each of us and it's a good thing." She went on to describe the broken bat at the Rockies game. The Minister's wife clapped a hand to her mouth.

"You poor dear, you could have been seriously injured!"

"Yes," answered the teenager. She was dressed in a simple, elegant, black dress with short sleeves and a red bow on each shoulder. "I don't know what possessed me to wear the armor shirt that day."

"What of the medallion?" asked the Prime Minister. "Are you still wearing it Ricardo?"

"No," said Great Grandfather. "I passed it on to Juan two years ago. He's the youngest by a minute, but I consider both twins to be the Wearer."

"Medallion?" questioned the older woman.

"Ahh," said her husband, "a silver medallion has been in their family for almost 500 years. It came from the Inca Empire after the conquistadors invaded and has been passed down from generation to generation. When Ricardo and my father became friends, we learned all about it. I think he trusted us because we're of Inca ancestry."

"Could I see it?" she inquired. A quick look from his relative kept Juan motionless.

"By all means," replied Great Grandfather smoothly, "but I think it would be best to wait until after we return from the site. Even in a restaurant like this, one never knows who might be watching, and the recent discovery in the mountains has generated a lot of interest."

"Of course," she said, wise to the intrigue that can surround any government official. "I understand completely; perhaps we could have tea when you return." Her husband leaned forward.

"Ricardo, you need to know that we've had a lot of trouble with bandits along the trail you'll be following. Many international climbing parties use it to access several popular climbing peaks in the area. A number of them have been robbed at gunpoint. Usually the thieves only take money, valuable GPS instruments and the like, but two groups were so stripped of gear they returned to Lima with literally only the clothes they were wearing. They were also frightened by the rough treatment they received. I'd like to send a couple of soldiers to protect you."

"That won't be necessary," replied Great Grandfather, "although I appreciate your concern. We have the medallion to warn us, as you know," he nodded toward Juan, "but I don't think we'll appear prosperous enough to attack. Furthermore, all our valuables will be left in the hotel's safe until we return." The Prime Minister wasn't satisfied.

"Let me give you a satellite phone then," he urged. "If you have trouble, I can dispatch one of our high-altitude helicopters to rescue you." Now it was the old man's turn to lean forward.

"That's one of the first things I purchased today and your personal number is already programmed into it."

CHAPTER 44
Trailhead

THE ROUGH AND ROCKY DIRT road ended abruptly in a tiny village consisting of six houses at the head of a long valley. To the west, enormous peaks dominated the skyline under a blue sky dusted with white clouds. After hours of bouncing along at a snail's pace, the packed Land Rover was covered with dust and its occupants eager to get out and stretch their legs.

"This is the end of the road," announced Great Grandfather as he switched off the engine. "From here we walk." As they stepped from the vehicle, a man rose from where he'd been sitting against the pink wall of a nearby house.

"Senor," he said, and began speaking rapidly in Spanish. The old man, dressed once again in jeans, plaid shirt, and work boots, listened closely and then replied with equal fluency. The local nodded and disappeared into his house.

"It seems some Japanese climbers came along yesterday and offered an exorbitant price to buy the llamas I'd agreed to rent for our trip," he explained. "Money is scarce here and Pedro couldn't refuse the offer, but he's gone to call a brother down valley who can supply us animals from his herd. It will take them a couple of hours to get here, so we might as well take our things out of the Land Rover and separate them into three loads." Pedro reappeared with news that his brother was on the way, then helped organize the gear into manageable packs for the animals. By the time they were done, a few curious kids had gathered to stare and soon Juan and Sophia were playing soccer with them on a nearby meadow.

By the time Pedro's brother appeared with the llamas it was too late to start, so they set up their two new tents on the erstwhile soccer field and had dinner with Pedro's family. When they emerged from the house, brilliant stars flooded the night sky, shedding enough light in the clear mountain air to cast their shadows as they walked to the tents.

"Wow, it's really cold," exclaimed Juan. "How high do you think we are?"

"We are close to 10,000 feet, I'd say," replied Great Grandfather. "Although Peru is considered to have a temperate climate, it is technically still winter here. We should be comfortable enough at night though; our sleeping bags are rated to –25°." Have you two got enough room in that tent?" Assured that they did, he disappeared into his small orange abode and soon all three were fast asleep in the warm bags.

CHAPTER 45

Clue

"Do mountain climbers use llamas on this trail?" asked Sophia, as they trudged up a series of switchbacks the second morning after leaving the village. Great rocky hills rose to either side as their route wound its way over ridges bisecting the wide valley they'd been following. "This would be brutal without these beauties," she added, fondly patting the nose of the llama she was leading. "We've done nothing but gain altitude since leaving Pedro's house."

"I'll bet we're close to 12,000 feet," ventured her brother.

"I doubt they use llamas on this trail," answered Great Grandfather. "It's not far to several climbable peaks. An expedition costs a lot of money and most serious climbers aren't wealthy; they're used to carrying their gear on shorter approaches. If it's a matter of weeks instead of just days, as in the Himalayas, then they will hire porters or animals to carry loads to where the real climbing begins."

"This is a well traveled path," noted Sophia. "You'd think someone would have discovered that carved block long before now."

"You're right," said the old man, who seemed completely unaffected by the exertion, despite his age. "Except the discovery wasn't made along this trail: the rock was found over two day's walk to the north." He gestured to their right, where a series of high gray mountains disappeared into the distance. "A severe storm forced a group of climbers to rappel off the mountain down a series of sheer cliffs no one had ever attempted. When they reached level ground, they were on the wrong side of the mountain and had to find their way back to this trail by trekking through uncharted territory. Apparently, it took some trial and error because the terrain is so rough. It was during that time they found the rock."

"How are *we* going to find it then?" asked Juan.

"Notice the small valleys that come into this one on both sides?" answered Great Grandfather. "We are to follow one of them on the north side. The climbers described a clue to indicate which one."

"Why only a clue?" asked Juan.

"Because two of the four climbers are professors at the University in Lima: a husband and wife. She teaches history and he anthropology. They realized the discovery might be important and wanted to make sure the site remained untouched until a proper archeological team reached it. There are always vandals and thieves looking for artifacts to sell on the black market. The professors didn't want to leave an obvious marker to point the way."

"How on earth are we allowed to go in before the Museum team, and what's the clue?" asked Sophia. It dawned on her that Peruvian officials must have incredible trust in her relative to disclose the clue and allow them in first.

"Well, I did a lot of field research on the Inca Empire when I was here as a young archaeologist," he replied vaguely. (It was only much later that the twins would learn his work was considered foundational to modern knowledge of the Incas.) "As for the clue, I'll know it when I see it," was all he would say.

It was late afternoon when Great Grandfather suddenly raised his hand and stopped walking. The valley had broadened to a quarter-mile width and the trail ran straight ahead toward an enormous massif of gray rock towering into the sky with four distinct peaks, clearly the target for some climbers. But the old man was staring across the dried grasses to a small side valley on their right. It was only 100 yards wide and perhaps 300 yards deep, ending in a steep rocky hillside. At the bottom of the hill was a jumble of boulders, but the twins could see nothing unusual: it looked like any of the numerous dead-end canyons they'd passed during the last two days. Their relative reached into his daypack for a small pair of binoculars and studied the area; after a minute he nodded and left the trail and headed across the yellowed grass toward the valley. Juan and Sophia hurried to lead the llamas after him.

"What is it, Great Grandfather?" asked Sophia. "What do you see?"

"Not much, but enough," came the reply, as the old man strode forward. When he stopped, 20 minutes later, the little group was at the foot of the hillside facing the clutter of rocks. "Notice anything?" he said. The twins knew better than to say "No," and studied the hillside for some minutes in silence. "To the left," hinted their relative.

"I don't see anything unusual," Sophia started to say but suddenly stopped. "Wait a minute." Her eyes widened. "Oh my gosh!" A minute later Juan saw it.

"You've got to be kidding!" he cried. "That boulder's not natural!" He pointed to a half-buried fragment at the bottom of the pile. "It's not natural: it's been shaped." Sure enough, a four-foot piece of rock stuck out of the ground like a slice of a gigantic melon. It had clearly been split apart, but the outer edge was unnaturally round and smooth.

"In its original shape, I'd say it was a perfectly round ball about eight feet high," said Great Grandfather. The twins stared at him as recognition began to dawn.

"But, there can't have been a road here; the rest of this jumble is untouched rock," said Juan.

"And the hillside is unbroken by any ledges," added Sophia, studying the terrain.

"Give Qist a little credit," replied the old man. "This was a deadly serious business: the conquistadors were out to ravage and destroy all Incas. My guess is we're standing on the remnants of cut and shaped pavers and rounded boulders, broken apart and buried under a natural-looking pile of rock, according to Qist's instructions. He probably had the stone balls rolled down the hill to make it easier for workmen to split them into pieces. This fragment was probably forced up by frost over the millennia. As for the stair road and flattened areas from which to launch the boulders against horsemen, all evidence was undoubtedly removed and the hill restored to its natural state. Qist's men must have done an excellent job, because the Spaniards didn't discover Pattiti for more than 10 years after they murdered the Emperor. Let's camp here tonight; there's a tiny spring and grass for the llamas. We'll tackle the hill tomorrow."

"Do you mean this is the site of the road into Pattiti?" cried Juan excitedly.

"Very possibly. We know there was an Inca road near the climber's trail, but it curved away south almost directly across from us." Ricardo pointed to a discernible break in the southern wall of hills. As he did so, a tiny wink of light caught his eye from a distant slope.

CHAPTER 46

Visitors

"Sophia," Juan breathed urgently in the near dark. "The medallion's hot." She awoke instantly.

"What time is it?"

"Almost 6:00, it's starting to get light. I've got to warn Great Grandfather."

"Be careful," she whispered. "I'll get my sling ready." The tent zipper seemed unnaturally loud as Juan lowered it. Outside, a dense fog had settled in overnight, not unusual for the area and normally gone by mid-morning. It did not, however, hide the six figures seated on rocks around their camp stove and cooking gear.

"Buenos dias," said one of the men, an automatic rifle gripped in one hand.

"Buenos dias," replied Juan. "But I'm afraid I don't speak Spanish too well."

"No problem," said one of the other men. "We speak English. Please sit on the ground. And tell the girl to come out." When Sophia appeared, she was directed to sit next to her brother.

"Now, before we wake up the old man, we want to know what you're doing up here," said the second man. All of them had dark beards and wore floppy-brimmed hats. They wore expensive down coats, but their pants were ragged above leather sandals. Each had a wicked looking machete at his waist and all were armed with automatic rifles and pistols. Two had handguns pointed at the twins.

"We're just hiking into the peaks," Juan said. "We're from the States but have Inca ancestry, so we wanted to see the terrain where they lived."

"That's a nice story," growled the man who had first spoken. "But it doesn't explain the fine satellite phone, expensive GPS locator, and high-quality binoculars we found in your packs. It's all new; not the kind of gear one takes on a casual trek. We're wondering what might be inside your tents."

"I'd be happy to show you: it's only clothing and sleeping bags," offered Juan, starting to rise. The medallion was so hot he knew they were in great danger.

"Sit down!" the man roared. "Get the old guy out here; he must be totally deaf not to have heard us." One of the men went to the orange tent and reached for the zipper but the flaps were open. He yelled in Spanish and stared about.

"He's not in there," snarled the bandit. "Where did he go?"

"I have no idea," said Juan. "We all went to sleep right after dinner."

"No matter," shrugged the leader. "After we're done with you, we'll pick him off as he tries to go down the trail. Now go over there and kneel, facing away from us, hands on your heads."

"You're going to kill us?" gasped Juan, comprehension dawning. "We've done nothing to you."

"No one will ever know; people are always getting lost and dying in these mountains. We don't like Americans, but we do like their gear and especially the expensive stuff that brings a good price."

"But this is my sister! She's never harmed anyone."

"Yeah, she's a beauty but time's running out. That Japanese group's coming back this morning and we need to pay them a visit. Put your hands on your heads and go kneel by that pile of rocks." When the twins hesitated, one of men jumped up and grabbed Sophia by her ponytail and yanked her clear off the ground.

"He said 'go kneel by that pile of rocks'," he screamed in her face. Juan threw himself at the man, only to receive a vicious blow to the face from the bandit's free hand. He fell backwards; his head struck the ground and everything went black.

CHAPTER 47

Bursts of Flame

"Juan, wake up. You've got to wake up!" Sophia's face swam into view above him, eyes wide with concern. "It's all over. Those men are tied up."

"Uhhh, what happened?" he managed as he raised himself to a sitting position, arms draped over bent knees, the smell of burned cloth in his nose. Sophia knelt in front of him and held out a cup of water.

"Drink this; it'll help clear your head." She pressed a damp cloth against his left cheek. "That guy really nailed you: you're going to have a huge shiner!" The cold water revived him and he noticed it was now full daylight and the fog had dissipated. Great Grandfather was busy breaking down their tents and loading the llamas; nearby six men lay side by side on the ground, arms and legs securely tied and gags over their mouths.

"What happened?" he asked, wincing at the soreness on the left side of his face.

"You're not going to believe it!" she exclaimed. "When you hit the ground there was a puff of smoke and a circular hole appeared in your clothing, exposing the medallion. Almost instantly, there was a flash and what looked like a teardrop-shaped flame shot out of the silver, striking the man who was holding me right in the chest. He flew backward 10 feet and his clothes burst into flames! He fell to the ground screaming and rolling around to put out the fire. Before I could move, one of the other men grabbed me and put a rifle to my forehead. I actually saw his finger start to tighten on the trigger, but another blob of flame smashed into his weapon, sending it spinning through the air and encasing his hand in fire! He squealed like a pig and fell to his knees, beating at the flames with his good hand. The other men were stock still, staring at the medallion in horror.

"The leader jumped up and ran to where you were lying. He aimed his pistol point-blank at your chest and yelled, 'I'll put an end to this!' Before he could act, twin streaks of flame erupted from the medallion and flashed along both sides of his head. He dropped his gun and clutched his ears, screaming. I could see blood dripping through his fingers!

"Then a ball of fire fell out of the fog and landed a few feet away, igniting the grass. The remaining three guys nearly jumped out of their skins and spun around, totally freaking out.

"There was this unearthly cry from the mist and one screeched, 'What was that!' only to stagger backwards, double over and slump to the ground. He had been hit so hard by a rock that it must have broken at least three ribs. The other two bandits swung this way and that, pointing their guns at the fog.

"One of them must have seen something that terrified him, because he suddenly emptied his entire clip of ammo into the fog and, a second later, the other guy did the same thing! They started fumbling for their spare clips but first one, then the other, crashed to the ground with a broken leg. I think they couldn't handle the fear and pain because they both passed out." Sophia giggled, but it was more to cover up the residual tension she was still feeling than to laugh.

"At that point, Great Grandfather strolled into the light of the fire, with a seriously scary mask over his head and shoulders. He looked like some sort of horror movie demon: a man's body with the head of a mountain lion. The other bandits had all been writhing around and howling in pain, but they went completely quiet, staring like their worst nightmare had come true. He collected their weapons and stood over them holding a rifle. The leader, hands still cupping what were left of his ears, struggled to sit up.

"'You don't fool me with that mask,' he yelled before Great Grandfather let off a long burst of shots into the dirt beside him. He lay back down with a moan and not one of them spoke or moved again. As Great Grandfather stood watch with the rifle, I tied and gagged them."

Juan got to his feet and approached Great Grandfather. "It looks like you were pretty busy while I was knocked out." He tried to grin, but the bruise twisted his face more like a grimace.

"I'm sorry about that bruise but I had to stay out of sight until I had an advantage over them," said his relative. "I spotted a flash of light in the hills on the other side of the valley yesterday," he went on, "and figured it would be prudent to separate myself from the camp in case we had visitors, but didn't want to alarm you. Unfortunately, there were more of them than I expected and they planned more than a robbery." He stared at the burned sides of the leader's head where his ears had been, "It's a good thing we had the medallion...."

CHAPTER 4 8
Mask

"THE ARMY HELICOPTER should have picked them up by now," said Great Grandfather. They were stopped for lunch several miles from the site of their camp.

"They'll be tended to and then imprisoned for a long, long time. When I called, the Prime Minister said there was one climbing group that completely disappeared two months ago. He thinks those men might have been responsible."

"They were flat-out going to kill us," said Juan for the umpteenth time. "I just couldn't believe it, but they were so matter-of-fact and the medallion was so hot I knew they were planning it!"

"Robbery isn't uncommon on the tourist trails, but those boys were prepared to go all-out and do away with us," agreed the old man.

"So, you had decided to spend the night outside, even before supper was over?" Sophia asked.

"Yup, I left right after you went to sleep," said her relative. "I stayed up in the rocks and got ready. When I saw that wink of light on the far slopes, I knew someone was glassing us. There was no need to bother you, so I just made sure I was prepared. The fog helped."

"Where did you learn to imitate a cougar scream?" Sophia wanted to know. "And what did you use to soak the cloth for the fireballs?"

"As water began to dry up in the canyons, we had a lot of cats coming for colts just like the one that Shadow killed when Tukor was a young man. We'd hear them scream at night and Dad taught me how to imitate it. I haven't used it for years; almost forgot how. As for the cloth, olive oil from our supplies worked just fine."

"Wait a minute," said Juan. "That mask, is it from the same cat Shadow stopped?"

"Yes, Tukor remembered the old jaguar mask Cuto and Rutu had used so effectively in the Popé and wanted something similar. He had it made, but never needed to wear it and gave it to me when he passed on the medallion. I've kept it all these years and, for some strange reason, brought it with me. I have no idea how to explain it: just grabbed it and threw it in my bag as we were leaving for the airport. Good thing I did."

"I'll say!" exclaimed Sophia. "When you walked out of the fog, they froze in shock. You should have seen their faces! It didn't last long, but adding the burst of automatic fire did the trick!

CHAPTER 49

Discovery

The highly sophisticated GPS device guided the little party and their llamas through a series of valleys and ridges deep into the Andes Mountains where no one would have suspected prior human presence. The twins continually expressed their amazement that there wasn't one clue pointing to the existence of the paved road and stone stairways that once existed.

Great Grandfather had a simple answer, "Give credit to Qist."

Four days after leaving the village, they emerged from a small canyon onto a large flat area strewn with rocks, bushes, and little hills. It was roughly rectangular, running east to west. At the west end, sheer cliffs rose to towering gray peaks, undoubtedly the escape route the climbers had rappelled down to escape the storm. An imposing ridge, at least 1,000 feet high, bordered the north side; on the southern border, jagged cliffs formed the base of a smaller ridge.

"Wow, this is sort of a little pocket of flat ground," said Juan. "How big do you think it is?"

"I'd estimate 600 or 700 yards long and 400 yards wide," replied his relative.

"Is it big enough for a city?" inquired Sophia.

"Absolutely," said Great Grandfather, "and I'm already seeing the evidence."

"What?" exclaimed Sophia in surprise. "What do you see?"

"Take a look at that piece of rock on the ground to your right. Notice anything unusual?" Sophia immediately saw that the rock had a precise corner on the side facing her."

"It's been cut to make a corner," she cried excitedly.

"Exactly. If I'm right, all the little hills you see are piles of rubble from the city, covered with dirt. I suspect that the entire area contains the remains of Pattiti, covered with earth to disguise the fact that a city existed here."

"But that's an incredible undertaking," observed Juan. "Dismantle a city and then bury it! Why would they do that?"

"Because they didn't want the conquistadors to discover where it had been," replied Great Grandfather. "My guess is that Qist left specific instructions about what to do if the city were found, and those instructions were carried out after his death. Don't forget, he was the Emperor's right-hand man."

"Yes, but why didn't he want the Spanish to know the city existed?"

"I think that's what we're here to find out," said the old archeologist. Juan and Sophia stared at each other in confusion, but their relative was already leading the llamas toward the north ridge to set up camp where a tiny waterfall indicated the presence of a stream.

The next morning they located the inscribed block that the climbers had stumbled on. Although the surface was badly worn, when Juan laid the medallion alongside the circular image, the two looked very similar. The twins were beside themselves with excitement, but Great Grandfather urged patience as his professional training came into play.

"The first job is to verify that we are in the right place," he explained. "We'll dig a series of pits to find out if I'm right about the city." By afternoon his theory had been proved correct: a foot below the surface in every pit, they encountered unmistakably hewn pieces of rock.

"When they finished doing this," the archeologist explained, "the surface of the valley would probably have appeared completely normal: rocky soil with a few small hills. Over time frost pushed up some of the rock, but even aerial photographs show this valley to be indistinguishable from the surrounding region."

"Have you studied those photographs?" asked Juan.

"The Museum sent me a couple to look at some years ago," said Great Grandfather in an offhand manner. In fact, he had been sent a massive package of pictures covering nearly 200 square miles of remote Andes valleys. "Now, the next step will be more fun. Let's see if we can locate any evidence of the stair-step road on the north ridge."

The following morning they began at one end of the ridge and walked along its base, studying the ground for any clue of the ancient road. The grass and dirt revealed nothing, but a third of the way along Sophia stumbled and nearly fell.

"I stubbed my toe on something," she cried, bending to stare at the ground. "There! A small edge of rock is poking up!" They all knelt down and Great Grandfather pulled out one of his small brushes. A minute's clearing of dirt revealed a corner of rock just at ground level. Retrieving shovels from camp, they carefully cleared the surrounding soil to reveal a perfectly smooth, flat step. Twenty minutes later another step had been cleared directly above it.

"It looks like they didn't dig the stair-step road out, just covered it with dirt," said Juan. "This is awesome!

Adzul's feet stepped on these stairs!" He looked up, "I wonder where the round boulders were stashed?"

"About halfway up, I'd say," answered Great Grandfather. "Want to check it out?"

"Of course!" was the twins' enthusiastic response.

"Take a shovel and poke through the dirt to find the stairs, although I'm sure they go straight up," advised their relative. Pushing the shovel down every few feet revealed that the stairs, made for llamas and humans, ascended straight up the hill. About halfway, Juan suddenly encountered no stone when he pushed down. He located the previous step, then tried again right above it but encountered nothing.

"This has got to be the flat area they cut in the hillside," ventured Sophia, "where the boulders were placed to roll down on horsemen. The Incas must have filled it in when they destroyed the city."

"I think you're right, and if we keep headed straight we should find the upper stairs," said Great Grandfather. "These roads went up and down over hills with no turns." Sure enough, 50 yards above, Juan's shovel hit rock again and they followed the route to the top of the ridge. Far below, a narrow valley twisted its way northward.

"Can you imagine Adzul running down wide stairs all the way to that valley?" wondered Juan. "You can see the curve where he was hidden from the riders and climbed the hillside to hide. To stand here and know what happened on this very hill centuries ago is awesome!" Lost in thought, the three made their way slowly back down the ridge and headed for camp.

CHAPTER 50

Vibrations

"Has the medallion reacted in any way since we've been here?" asked Great Grandfather the next morning as they sat around the camp stove eating oatmeal.

"I was going to mention that," replied Juan. "Ever since we walked into this valley, I've felt the slightest tingle where the medallion touches my skin. It's been so light I didn't say anything, because I thought it might be static electricity at this high altitude, or something, but when we discovered the stair-step road it seemed to get stronger. This morning it has returned to the faintest tingle." The old man was silent for a few minutes.

"I think we should conduct some tests," he said finally.

"What kind of tests?" asked Juan.

"If you think about our family's history with the medallion, in particular during the past couple of years, I believe it's no coincidence that the three of us are in this valley before any team arrives from the Museum. It's revealed more to the two of you than to any other Wearer. We're here and now the medallion is tingling. I think somehow it's guiding us."

"What should we do?" inquired the youth.

"I think the three of us should stroll around this valley and see if the tingling increases at any spot," replied Great Grandfather. "I know it sounds unprofessional, after what you now know of my work in archaeology, but call it instinct. Plus, the medallion behaves like no other known artifact. Let's start where we know the city actually was, just below the stair road up the ridge." The twins nodded and hurried to wash the breakfast bowls.

For nearly an hour, they walked slowly back and forth over what Great Grandfather estimated to be the area occupied by the city. Next, they followed the base of the north ridge to its end. Juan reported no increase in the tingling. At the western end of the valley they passed the sheer cliffs down which the climbers had rappelled, but there was still no change.

"Let's walk along the south wall," suggested the archeologist. "The early family history says nothing about it but perhaps there's a connection." The southern side of the valley consisted of cliffs rising vertically for nearly 30 feet before rounding into a gentle slope ascending a low ridge. At the bottom of these cliffs were jumbled shards and slabs of granite, which had split from the walls over the millennia. The trio hadn't gone more than 25 yards when Juan abruptly stopped .

"Something's going on," he declared in a hushed voice. "The medallion is actually starting to vibrate!" He pulled the silver from beneath his clothes and held it in front of him.

"Juan!" exclaimed his sister excitedly. "I can see black smoke through the hole!" She pressed close and both peered at the medallion. Great Grandfather stepped beside them and stared at the square hole, but only saw the cliff on the other side of it.

"The smoke's clearing," murmured Juan.

"Great Grandfather, can you see them?" Sophia asked excitedly.

"No, I just see the cliff before us. The revelation is for the two of you, but describe what you're seeing." There was silence for a moment as the twins focused on the medallion, and then Juan lowered his hand.

"It's gone," he said, "and the medallion isn't vibrating anymore. In fact, it's not even tingling."

"People... We saw people coming and going through a large doorway. The ones going in were carrying things and the ones coming out were empty-handed," the words tumbled out of his sister. "It was pretty dark outside, but inside the door it was lighter and I think I saw torches."

"From what we know, they must have been Incas," Juan added. "Most wore wool caps with ear flaps, sleeveless tunics, and sandals."

"Almost all of them had what looked like gold ear plugs," interjected Sophia.

"What were they carrying?" asked Great Grandfather.

"Some had what seemed to be large baskets or boxes; they must have been heavy, because it took two people to carry them. Others had what looked like rolls of metal and I saw one person with what looked like a small piece of furniture," said Juan. "But the scene ended so fast we couldn't take in much detail." Sophia nodded in agreement.

"I suggest we mark this spot," said their relative, bending to assemble a rock cairn with some of the stones scattered around. "Then let's continue along the ridge to where we first entered the valley. I want to see if there is any further reaction from the medallion."

When they reached the small canyon through which they'd first entered the area, Juan reported he'd felt nothing more from the silver piece.

CHAPTER 51
Rockfall

Rᴇᴛᴜʀɴɪɴɢ ᴛᴏ ᴛʜᴇ ꜱᴛᴏɴᴇ ᴄᴀɪʀɴ, the archeologist sat down and studied the cliff for a long time, Juan and Sophia beside him. The accumulated rock-fall from hundreds of years reached approximately eight feet up the face. Above it a gray rock face rose more than 20 feet, at a slight backward angle, to where it met dried grass and a gentle slope to the low ridgeline.

"Clever, very clever," remarked Great Grandfather after many minutes. "Let's go back to camp and get some tools." He rose and set off at a brisk pace for the tents.

"What's clever?" asked Juan as he and his sister struggled to catch up.

"You'll see," was all the old man would say. When they reached camp, he suggested they all have some food because the afternoon was going to be taken up with hard work. When that was accomplished, they set about collecting a couple of pickaxes, a shovel, and an old leather case containing Great Grandfather's brushes and chisels. "I'm glad we had the llamas to carry this gear," the old man remarked offhandedly as he extracted a small but stout come-along (a winch-like device to pull heavy objects) from one of the packs. Once again, the twins stared at each other; they had privately thought their relative was crazy to bring along such an item and wondered how he would use it. When they got back to the cairn and put the tools down, he began to explain.

"Look at the cliff face directly in front of us," he said. "Do you see anything unusual?" They stared at the granite surface.

"No, honestly, I don't," replied Juan.

"Nor I," answered Sophia.

"All right, now look either 20 feet to the right or left. What do you see?"

"The same rock surface, with cracks and splits, from where pieces have flaked off. No, wait, it's NOT the same!" the girl cried. "The part in front of us has no cracks or splits: the surface is unbroken from the top of the rubble for about five feet. It's rough, but there are no fissures or splits. Above that, and for several feet to either side, the face of the cliff has little fractures everywhere. Unless you looked closely, you'd never notice the smooth section."

"But there's rubble under it, just like the rest of the cliff," Juan started to argue, then abruptly stopped. "Unless it was put there on purpose," he said as light dawned. "But why would that section be smooth?"

"To mark a location, for someone who knew what to look for." his sister pronounced. Great Grandfather grinned.

"You guys might make good archeologists some day! Let's see if we can move some of this debris."

As they set to work on the pile of rubble, they found that one person could carry almost every rock, or rock fragment, yet the pile was arranged in such a way as to give the appearance of much larger pieces haphazardly strewn on top of one another. In three hours, they had cleared the foot of the cliff for a 40-foot stretch. All that remained was an oblong slab of granite, partially buried in the dirt, which looked as though it had split off from the cliff. In fact, there was an identically shaped scoring of the rock face showing the outline of where it had come away. It appeared to have been an irregularly shaped five-foot-wide slab of rock, about eight feet tall, that had separated from the cliff and fallen to the ground.

"What say you?" inquired Great Grandfather as they gathered around the slab.

"It looks pretty natural, but I'm suspicious," said Juan.

"You should be. Look at this." The old archeologist moved close to the cliff and ran his finger along the edge of the split supposedly made by the slab falling away. "There are tiny marks along the whole edge of this break. Someone either cleverly cut the slab out of the cliff or fashioned the slab and cut its image into the rock."

"Either way, it must have been done with incredible skill because it looks exactly like that piece fell off into the dirt," said Sophia.

"That's what they wanted us to think, right?" guessed Juan.

"Right," answered Great Grandfather. "Now, all we have to do is move the slab."

It took some doing, because the rock was nearly a foot thick, but they finally dug out one corner sufficiently to attach the come-along. With the other end of its cable around a large boulder nearby, they took turns pulling the handle. It was hard work because of the sheer weight of the slab, but bit by bit it began to slide from its resting spot to expose not the dirt they expected, but empty space beneath. On hands and knees, the three peered into the opening.

"It's a stone staircase," exclaimed Sophia in awe. "With stone walls on either side."

"I wonder where it goes?" questioned Juan. "There were no stairs where those people were carrying the baskets and bundles."

CHAPTER 52

Dead End

"I'M NOT GOING TO BE ABLE to sleep tonight," rued Sophia. "I'm so excited to see what we'll find at the bottom of those stairs."

It had taken the rest of the afternoon to drag the slab clear of the empty shaft and completely expose the stairway. They were rather surprised to see that it wasn't steep: broad, dusty stairs descended at a gentle angle between smooth stone walls. Great Grandfather had decided to delay further exploration until morning.

"If there's bad air down there, we want to give it a chance to escape," he'd explained.

Now, as they ate their tasty freeze-dried stroganoff dinner, conversation was rampant with speculation about the stairway. Juan thought it might be some kind of a trap designed to lure conquistadors to their deaths. Sophia argued that slab and stair were so perfectly designed and camouflaged that there must be more to it than a death trap. Their relative didn't offer much analysis, but all three agreed that the medallion was at last revealing its secret.

"We'd never have discovered the stairs if it hadn't vibrated at that spot," stated Juan. "After 500 years in the family's care, I think we're going to find out why Qist wanted the medallion preserved."

"I agree," said Great Grandfather. "I've always said I thought you were the ones chosen to reveal its secret. But I suggest we head for the tents before we talk the night away. The temperature is dropping fast and those warm sleeping bags will feel good." The night sky was so brilliant with starlight that the snow-capped peaks to the west could clearly be seen as they made their way the few yards to where the little domed structures were pitched.

"No wonder Great Grandfather loved traveling all over the world to explore ancient ruins," said Juan as he and Sophia paused outside their blue tent. "This is so awesome!" Despite declaring that she was too excited to rest, Sophia was asleep within minutes.

The distinctive sound of the hissing campstove woke the twins before it was fully light. As memory of the previous afternoon's discovery flooded back, both scrambled out of their bags and into heavy fleece pants and down parkas because the outside temperature was close to freezing. Great Grandfather was sitting on a rock beside the stove, a coffee cup warming his hands.

"Good morning. There's more coffee in the pot," he said, nodding at the stove. "I put cream and sugar on the table." The "table" was a chunk of building stone they'd found which had a flat surface perfect for holding cooking gear.

"Morning," replied Juan. "When do we explore the stairs?"

"Well, it's just starting to get light and I don't want one of us to break a neck falling down that hole," chuckled the archeologist. "Why don't we have breakfast, clean up, and go over there in an hour. It won't be warm, but we'll at least have some sunlight to work with. I would suggest we take headlamps. There's no telling how deep it is."

An hour later, three shafts of light pierced the dark stairwell.

"It's not deep at all," exclaimed Sophia as they followed their relative down the wide steps to a landing. "We've only come down eight or nine feet." The floor, walls, and ceiling of the landing were made of fitted blocks and at its far end a stone hallway extended away into the dark.

"Where do you suppose it goes?" asked Sophia.

"Let's find out," said Great Grandfather. "It leads away from the cliff, perhaps there's some underground structure ahead." He took the lead, light from his headlamp piercing the black.

"This is incredible," said Juan in a low voice. "From the ground above, nobody would have the slightest idea this existed." They walked for five minutes, the hallway running straight as an arrow.

"Well, I'll be," murmured the old archeologist suddenly halting. Ten feet in front of him, the hall came to an end. A few square blocks of stone were scattered about and floor, walls, and ceiling were in various stages of completion. Directly ahead was a solid wall of dirt. Clearly, work had been brought to a halt before the hallway was finished.

"They never finished it!" exclaimed Juan. "Maybe the conquistadors showed up before they could."

"I wonder what they had in mind?" said Sophia, clearly disappointed. Great Grandfather stood, sweeping the headlamp from side to side, examining the unfinished work. Finally he swung around.

"If they were interrupted, why would they have taken such care to hide the excavation?" he asked, walking purposefully back toward the stairs.

CHAPTER 53

Stair Tread

THE STAIRWAY WAS BRIGHT with sunlight when they reached it. Minutes passed as the old man studied it. "Let's examine every square inch of this shaft and stairs," he said. "Something tells me there is more here than meets the eye." An hour later, Sophia beckoned the other two.

"Look at this!" she exclaimed. "I may have found something." The three had been examining areas of the stairwell assigned by Great Grandfather. Juan had the whole left wall and half the ceiling. Great Grandfather had taken the corresponding right wall and ceiling; Sophia was to examine the stairs and floor. She was on hands and knees at the bottom of the stairs, using a brush to clear away centuries of dust from the top of the last step. On the right-hand side, 12 inches from where the stair met the wall, there was an almost invisible line across the step. "Every tread is made from a single piece of stone," she explained. "But this one has a line on it from the riser to the edge of the step." Great Grandfather bent and peered closely at the line.

"If I'm not mistaken," he declared, "the top of this step is made of two pieces of rock fitted together so well that they're almost indistinguishable, particularly with some dust to hide it. The work is very precise."

"What does it mean?" asked Juan.

"I don't know, but we'll need some tools."

A trip back to camp yielded a lightweight titanium hammer and several extremely thin chisels made of the same material. The archeologist first took a cloth and carefully wiped every particle of dust from the line. He then placed the blade of one chisel in the crack at the edge of the stair, where it met the riser coming up from the landing, and tapped lightly. The blade didn't move.

"The Incas really knew how to work rock!" he exclaimed. "The separate piece you found in this tread is so tightly fitted it won't budge. Hold the chisel in place please, Sophia, I'm going to start another one halfway to the side wall." Taking another chisel, he placed it against the crack and tapped with the hammer. Again, the blade didn't move. "OK, we'll try a third chisel exactly where the tread meets the wall.

It's getting crowded, but see if you can reach an arm in and hold the second chisel, Juan." With each twin holding a blade, Great Grandfather fitted a third into the crack where the tread and riser met the sidewall, and tapped. This time the thin blade penetrated the crack by a millimeter.

"Ahah, progress," murmured the old man. "If you don't mind, Juan, see if you can hold chisels two and three in place while I do the tapping." By lying along the next stair above, the youth was able to accomplish this feat as his relative moved between the three chisels, rapping each lightly in turn. After several tries, the middle chisel began to penetrate the crack. "Now, for chisel number one," said the archeologist. After several blows, the blade penetrated ever so slightly.

"Great Grandfather!" cried Sophia excitedly. "The piece has moved slightly up from the rest of the tread!" Indeed, the stair now showed a tiny edge where the rock had been pried up.

"It's so well made that only pressure from all three blades will lift it," explained her relative. It took another 45 minutes of work before the edge of the piece had tilted above the rest of the tread by an inch. "We need the pry bar now," said the old man, reaching for the short tool he had brought from the packs. It, too, was made of the lightest and finest metal available. Placing one end into the gap, he gently pried; repeating the process at the three points he'd applied the chisels. The rock was so well fitted that it took another 45 minutes to pivot the 12-inch-wide piece so that it tilted 45 degrees above the riser.

"I don't think the piece is going to come out," said Great Grandfather. "Let's all push on it and see if we can get it completely upright." With Sophia and the archeologist kneeling and Juan leaning over them from behind, all three strained against the rock until it was tipped upright against the riser to the next step.

"The piece is only an inch thick at most! How can it be so hard to raise?" cried Juan.

"It's beautifully fitted between the wall and the rest of the tread," described Great Grandfather. "The pressure from those two points causes the problem. The craftsman made sure it would be extremely difficult to pry it apart. But look what's below!" The headlamps revealed what looked like the corner of a piece of smooth granite, six inches below the tread.

"No way!" Sophia almost shouted, "No way!" Juan just stared.

"You're right," he finally said. "It's what we saw the mason making."

"The scene in the medallion?" asked the archeologist. Juan nodded.

"See the circular shape with raised symbols and the square knob sticking up? If you slipped the medallion over it, I think it would fit perfectly."

CHAPTER 54

Upside Down

THE THREE STARED IN hushed silence at the raised image on the granite for several minutes. "Are you ready?" asked Great Grandfather finally. The twins looked at each other and nodded.

"We're ready," they said simultaneously. Juan pulled the leather strap over his head and lifted the medallion from under his shirt.

"Funny," he said absently, "the tingling completely disappeared after we stopped at this section of the cliff." He reached for his knife. "Has the strap ever worn out, Great Grandfather?"

The old man shook his head. "Not as far as I know. It's part of the great mystery of the medallion."

"This is really hard to do," Juan muttered, holding the strap in one hand and knife in the other. He slid the blade across the leather and severed it. "We'll keep the strap safely at home." But there was an audible gasp from his sister.

"It's gone!" she cried. And so it was: when her brother looked at his hand, only the piece of silver was there. He turned shocked eyes to the archeologist.

"The strap served its purpose," said the old man. "It came from this valley in the first place…." Juan nodded in understanding and moved to kneel over the hole.

"Wait," said his sister. "Make sure you put the medallion down with matching symbols on the underside; each side of it is different." Her brother studied the piece of granite and turned the medallion over.

"This is the matching surface," he said, pausing for a minute with his hand over the chiseled rock. "Well, here we go," he announced, slipping the silver down over the square peg until the symbols cut into it fitted over the matching raised markings.

Nothing happened for a minute and then the granite suddenly dropped from sight and a great rumbling noise began. Dust poured out of the hole and rose along both edges of the stairway. All three scrambled back to stand on the landing because the stairs had started to move. They watched in fascination as the top of the staircase began to slowly drop into a walled shaft beneath it, where there should have been solid dirt.

"The whole stair is carved from a single block of stone, but made to look like pieces fitted together, except for the small section we uncovered," exclaimed Great Grandfather in awe as the bottom step pivoted against the landing while the upper steps dropped lower and lower until the whole piece was aimed downward. With a "thud" the stairs stopped moving and the rumbling ceased. Facing them was a stairway now descending from the landing toward the cliff, in the opposite direction of the hallway.

"The risers have become treads," observed Juan excitedly, flashing his headlamp down the steps. "But the medallion's gone."

"No, it's not," replied Sophia calmly. "It's in my hand." Sure enough, the piece of silver was gripped in her right hand. The other two stared in amazement.

"How did that happen?" said her brother finally.

"I'm not sure," she acknowledged, "but when the granite dropped, the medallion flew off the peg and into my hand." The two of them looked at Great Grandfather.

"Don't look at me," he said. "I don't know what's going on. But I've always said I thought both of you should be considered the Chosen Ones. Now, shall we go down and see where this new stair goes?" They slowly descended to another landing, headlamps revealing fitted stone walls on either side and a similarly made ceiling above.

CHAPTER 55

The Door

"From the surface, we're about 18 to 19 feet down when you consider the depth of the first landing before the stair pivoted, right" asked Juan when they reached the level floor.

"Yes," answered the archaeologist, "but this landing doesn't go anywhere." Facing them, six feet away, was a smooth rock wall.

"Do you suppose it's another dead end, like the tunnel?" asked Juan. "This looks like the face of the cliff below ground level."

"It is the face of the cliff as far as I can tell, but I doubt it's a dead end," replied Great Grandfather.

"I think you're right," said Sophia, moving to the right hand wall where it met the cliff. "Look at this." There, at waist height, etched in the last stone block before hallway met cliff, was another raised symbol and peg the size of the medallion. Once again, in the light of their headlamps the three stared at the carving in silence.

"Try the medallion," said Sophia, handing the silver to her brother. "But I think these symbols match the opposite side." Juan stepped forward and reached his hand toward the square peg, but it stopped six inches away. He strained but couldn't move his hand forward.

"I can't place the medallion over the peg," he exclaimed in frustration, "It feels like there's an invisible wall between it and me."

"That's because you're not meant to place it," said Great Grandfather with sudden insight. "Your sister is supposed to." He directed his headlamp at Sophia and smiled, "Go ahead, sweetheart, it's your turn." Juan instantly knew his relative was right and pressed the silver into her hand.

"Go for it. You're the other half of this team!"

Sophia hesitated for a moment, then stepped forward and focused her headlamp on the wall. Making sure she had the matching symbols facing the carving, she reached out her hand and smoothly slid the medallion over the peg. Nothing happened. They all stared in consternation. It was left to Great Grandfather to solve the mystery.

"Twist it," he suggested. Sophia placed her fingers on the silver and tried to turn it toward the cliff face, but it wouldn't move. "The other way," murmured the old man. When she moved her fingers to the right, the medallion and the carving spun a half circle before stopping. Immediately, there was an enormous crash and the rock face in front of them started to ponderously slide to the left. Further and further it went until it disappeared into a slot in the left wall. Facing them was an opening six feet wide and eight feet high. Beyond was darkness.

CHAPTER 56

Cavern

"It's gone!" Sophia cried. "The medallion's gone! As soon as it stopped turning, it disappeared! My fingers felt only the peg and raised symbols." She was ready to cry. Juan grabbed her hand and Great Grandfather put an arm around her shoulders.

"That's because its purpose was accomplished," he said quietly. "Its secret has finally been revealed. It was a key to trigger the stairway to drop and to open this door. It took both of you to complete the task. Don't be sad, this is why our family have been custodians of the medallion for all these centuries. Let's go and see what's inside."

When they walked through the opening they had the immediate feeling they were in a very large space, borne out as headlamps revealed a vast cavern. It was so large the walls to either side were hardly visible and they couldn't see the far end. The irregular ceiling was over 20 feet high.

"Did they make this?" gasped Sophia, her feeling of loss overcome by awe.

"I don't think so," replied Great Grandfather after he'd swept his light about. "The floor is certainly man-made, you can see the fitted rock, but the walls and ceiling look natural. I suspect there is a crack or fissure, which the Incas found, that leads into this cave. It must have been too small for an entrance, but undoubtedly served as a vent to keep the air clean. When they decided to make use of the space, they cut the doorway through the cliff face."

"They were obviously going to build something here because they left a huge pile of rubble," said Juan, as his light swept over enormous mounds of dust-coated material covering the floor. Maybe they were going to build some kind of underground refuge to hide people from the conquistadors."

"Perhaps," said Great Grandfather, walking to the closest pile of debris. Plucking an object from the floor, he brushed it with one hand, and then applied the sleeve of his anarak to polish it. Held to the light from his headlamp, the object threw off a reflection.

As the twins drew close, they could see he was holding a shiny yellow plate.

"Is that gold?" whispered Sophia, after a moment of stunned silence.

"I believe it is. In fact, I think there's no rubble at all, but everything on the floor of this cave is made of gold." No one spoke as they stared at the enormous collection of objects, five feet high in places, stretching away into darkness. "There are countless legends about lost Inca gold, hidden from the conquistadors," Great Grandfather continued. "But, after centuries of searching, no one has ever found it and the legends have come to be regarded as myth."

"It's no myth," said Juan somberly.

"So that's what we saw through the medallion," exclaimed Sophia. "People carrying things through that doorway into this cave." Great Grandfather bent over to pick up what look like frayed strands of rope.

"There were probably woven baskets and boxes stacked as high as they could reach," he said, "but over the centuries the reeds disintegrated and spilled the gold, creating these enormous piles. You mentioned rolls being carried in. I'll wager the archeologists will find they are thin sheets of gold removed from the sides of buildings. Remember a couple of years ago I told you that the Incas didn't value gold as money but as a symbol of prestige. They had the technology, before Europeans did, to refine it into thin sheets to reflect the sun."

"This is awesome! Can we explore further?" asked Juan, completely energized by the enormity of what they'd found.

"I think it best not to disturb things," replied the old man. "It will be important for the archaeologists to catalogue and record everything as it is, piece by piece. They'll bring generators and lights and we can hang around for a while to watch. But right now we need to go back to camp; I've got a call to make."

CHAPTER 57

Explanations

"Several helicopters will be here in the morning," Great Grandfather announced an hour later as he put down the satellite phone. "The Prime Minister himself is coming, with a detachment of soldiers and a team from the Museum. He said he wants to be the first Peruvian of Inca descent to see the cavern. We're to personally escort him."

"Wow," said Juan. "That's cool!"

"And they're not wasting any time getting here," added Sophia.

"Nor should they," said the old man. "This will be one of the greatest archaeological discoveries since

Carter found the tomb of Tutankhamen. The site needs to be properly protected as research goes forward."

"Can you imagine the excitement at the Museum?" mused Juan. "I'll bet those people are going crazy!"

"Did you tell him to bring ladders?" Sophia asked.

"Yes, of course," laughed her relative, "as you know, the PM is a little portly; he might have trouble getting in and out of that first landing without one." The return to camp had taken some creativity since there was now only an empty shaft where the stairs had originally been. Standing on Juan's shoulders, Sophia had scrambled out and returned with a length of climbing rope she found stashed in one of the packs. Tying one end securely to a boulder, she'd dropped the other to the landing; Juan and Great Grandfather had "walked" up the sidewall leaning back on the rope for support.

"So, Great Grandfather," probed Juan, "what's your take on all of this?" The old archeologist, sitting on a rock, clasped his hands around one knee and leaned back to stare at the sky with the expression the twins knew so well. They had seen it countless times as he traveled mentally into the past to recount family history.

"You'll remember that Qist was personal advisor to Emperor Atahualpa, who had a 375 square foot room filled with gold to buy his freedom from the conquistador, Francisco Pizarro. When Pizzaro then treacherously murdered the Emperor, I believe Qist realized the conquistadors' insatiable lust for gold could never be satisfied and fled the court with his young son. Retreating to the remote city of Pattiti, he put masons to work cutting an entrance into the cavern. At the same time he had the road leading to the city obliterated, to hide all traces of the population's existence.

"An order went out for people to bring their gold to Pattiti, to be hidden until the conquistadors were driven out. As the Emperor's aide, he possessed great authority and the Incas undoubtedly complied over the next few years. By the time the Spaniards finally discovered the city, the cavern had been filled and sealed, the entrance disguised, and the medallion created. This would explain his final words for his son to flee the Empire and preserve the medallion. Probably only Qist and a few trusted workers knew the piece of silver was actually a key. What I believe you saw in June was the creation of one of he triggering mechanisms for the medallion to lower the stairs and open the cavern door.

"Qist must have been obsessed with preventing the conquistadors from finding the gold. That southern cliff face is completely innocuous unless you know what to look for. The rubble covering the stairs was ingeniously designed to look completely natural. Only if you moved the big flat rock would you discover the stairs and they lead to a long tunnel that appears to have been abandoned before completion. And even if the conquistadors found and opened the square section of stone on the bottom step, they would need the medallion to trigger the stairs to pivot and expose the door to the cavern."

"How do you think the stair and door mechanisms worked?" asked Juan.

"Probably, it was controlled by some heavy counterweights that were delicately balanced with a hair-trigger release—particularly in the case of the door. The museum people may be able to figure it out in time." replied Great Grandfather before continuing.

"There must have been instructions for the people to wipe out the first conquistador party to discover Pattiti, then raze every building to the ground, disguise the ruins, and flee. The strategy seems to have been executed perfectly: the location might never have been discovered if those climbers hadn't gotten into trouble on the mountain. But when they did, all the pieces were in place for us to unlock the medallion's secret."

"Unbelievable," exclaimed Juan, looking at his sister, "do you realize the medallion was given to Adzul not far from where we're sitting? After all this time, it finally came into our hands and required each of us to be a part of the solution. Actually, it took all three of us because we couldn't have done it without Great Grandfather's connections and experience in archaeology."

"Not to mention his skill with the sling. We definitely wouldn't have survived the bandits without him!" added Sophia, grinning at the old man. "He's the best!" For the first time in their experience with him, Great Grandfather blushed.

Epilogue

THE TWINS AND GREAT GRANDFATHER stayed for several days to escort the Prime Minister into the cavern and to observe the initial work of the museum team. Upon returning to Colorado, they were met at the Denver airport by a horde of reporters wanting information about the news flashed around the world of one of the greatest treasure discoveries in modern times. Over the next six weeks there were interviews with all the major TV networks and countless visits with talk show hosts all over the country. During that time, the twins learned that their modest gardening relative had been, in his time, a world renowned archaeologist with many original discoveries to his credit.

Six months later, the three were flown to Lima by the Peruvian government. In a ceremony at the Government Palace, they were each granted The Order of the Sun, the highest possible Peruvian award for civil merit. In his presentation speech, the Prime Minister identified it as the oldest civilian award in the Americas, established in 1821.

"This building was originally constructed by the Conquistador Francisco Pizarro in 1535," he concluded. "It is the proper setting to express the gratitude of all Peruvian citizens for the discovery of Inca riches thought to be lost to the world, and to present this award to three individuals who trace their lineage to those who originally hid the treasure." Thunderous applause erupted throughout the chamber.

In the years that followed, Juan and Sophia graduated with high honors from high school and followed Great Grandfather's example by enrolling at the University of Denver. One of his proudest moments was seeing them receive their diplomas in an outdoor ceremony one mild summer morning. Following graduate work at DU, they pursued their Doctor of Archaeology degrees from the University of Aberdeen in Scotland, graduating in 2010.

Today, Juan is on the upper reaches of the Nile researching a legendary treasure lost during the period when Ethiopian Pharaohs ruled Egypt. Sophia is in Kazakhstan, on the Ukok Plateau, seeking a trove of

Greek artifacts and Chinese silk reportedly hidden there by the Pazyryk Ice Maiden (whose mummy was discovered in 1993). Through satellite phones they are in constant contact with each other.

Made in the USA
Middletown, DE
29 June 2020